Public Reading Followed by Discussion

Danielle Mémoire

PUBLIC READING
FOLLOWED BY DISCUSSION

Translated from the French by K. E. Gormley

DALKEY ARCHIVE PRESS

Dallas / Dublin

Originally published by P.O.L (Paris) as *Lecture publique suivie d'un débat* in 1994

Copyright © by Danielle Mémoire in 2019

Translation copyright © by K. E. Gormley, 2019.

First Dalkey Archive edition, 2020.

CIP Data available upon request.

www.dalkeyarchive.com

Dallas / Dublin

Printed on permanent/durable acid-free paper.

Contents

Preface: Reading Aloud
Warren Motte

You are about to discover Danielle Mémoire's *Public Reading Followed by Discussion*—or perhaps you have already read it, and you saved this preface and the translator's introduction for later. Either way, you may be interested to know a bit more about Mémoire, since this is the first of her major texts to be brought into English. Born in 1947, she launched her literary career in 1984 with a novel entitled *Dans la tour* (In the Tower). Since then, twenty of her books have appeared at the Éditions P.O.L (two periods rather than three in that name, please, for the sake of symmetry), a Parisian publishing house founded by Paul Otchakovsky-Laurens, and known for the boldness and discernment of its catalogue. Danielle Mémoire thus belongs to a generation of French writers who had learned the lessons of the *nouveau roman*, and of other literary experiments in its wake, and who inherited a horizon of writerly possibility that was significantly broadened. I'm thinking here of figures like Jean Echenoz, Jacques Jouet, Marie Redonnet, Jean-Philippe Toussaint, Marie NDiaye, Christian Gailly, and Antoine Volodine (to name just a few), people who helped to make the 1980s such a fruitful decade for prose narrative in France.

Over the course of her career, Danielle Mémoire has distinguished herself by the rigor of her writing, a rigor one might call classical, if such a term did not sound so dissonant in our vexed present. People interested in that effect might consider *Mes oncles, II* (2004, My Uncles, II), which wagers on a language that is, by any standard, heavily "refined." Or one might point to the present text, for that matter—and I would like to note that K. E. Gormley has rendered Mémoire's linguistic idiosyncrasies with a great deal of adroitness, resourcefulness, and tact; briefly stated, this translation shines. Unlike certain other writers known for their attention to highly polished style, however, Mémoire is consistently attentive to her reader. Her writing is generous in its attitude toward us; it provides us with what the critic Ross Chambers called "room for maneuver"; it offers us a place to *do something*. She presumes that we readers are not passive vessels into which literary meaning is to be poured, but rather smart, active, engaged folks who are both willing and able to participate in the construction of literary meaning. Danielle Mémoire is moreover a particularly gifted sculptor—and wrangler—of characters. While that talent is on display in all of her texts (including the one you're holding in your hands), it is especially evident in books like *Les Personnages* (2000, Characters) or *Les Auteurs* (2017, Authors), where fictional characters multiply like sex-crazed chinchillas, each one demanding our attention, and indeed our care, granted that each one has a story to tell. Among those characters, and speaking of the "author," Mémoire often limns a portrait of the artist in her novels, one that is heavily ironized with regard to any real-life writer one might be tempted to recognize, but who plays a significant role in the way we readers think about the authorial intentions that subtend the text. Such is the case in *Fautes que j'ai faites* (2001, Mistakes I've Made), for example, a novel wherein a writer—or several writers—look back at texts written in the past, with a distinctly jaundiced gaze. Such is also the case in Mémoire's latest book, *Le Rendez-vous de la marquise* (2019, The Marquise's Meeting), which has a lot to say about how writers inhabit their fictions, and wherein we are pleased to encounter once again certain characters whom we first met in some of Mémoire's previous books.

There is a marked dimension of theatricality in many of Mémoire's novels; and indeed she herself has commented on that effect on more than one occasion, suggesting that she feels that something is being *played out* on the stage of her books, even if the reasons accounting for that dynamic remain perplexing to her. If one is willing to consider language as character, it is demonstrably true that her novels put language on stage and cause it to perform for us. Furthermore, in view of the fact that theater is fundamentally involved in *play*, after all, it is useful to imagine Mémoire's works as examples of ludic literature. They are books that invite us to play, to give free rein to our ludic instinct, in close, collaborative articulation with the author. Mémoire, for her part, makes significant gestures toward us in order to enlist us in a playful reading. She uses humor, and irony, parody, and authorial asides; she winks at us frequently, either in reasonably subtle manners or in ways that are utterly (and amusingly) elephantine, in her efforts to gain our complicity. For, to her enduring credit, she envisions her reader as a partner, as someone who has chosen to enter the fictional world she has created, and who is interested in doing something more than just admiring the scenery. Mémoire proposes that world to us as one that is significantly permeable with regard to our own "real" world; she argues that we can migrate fluidly, usefully, and pleasurably from one world to the other, and back again, simply by exercising our imagination, and without the feeling of guilt that such metaleptic gestures often occasion in certain souls (those who are perhaps in any case looking for excuses to feel guilty). The shifting narrative terrain in Mémoire's worlds does tend to keep us on our toes, however, as agile as we may imagine ourselves to be; and the way that stories give rise to other stories, often nesting within each other like a set of Russian matryoshka dolls, may cause our head to spin from time to time, it's true. Yet that's what we signed up for, in a sense, and it is legitimate to imagine those very local moments of bewilderment as the spice in the savory literary dishes that Danielle Mémoire cooks up for us, dishes that will satisfy readerly appetites of very different kinds.

Introduction
K. E. Gormley

LIKE THAT OF BORGES, Nabokov, and Lewis Carroll, Danielle Mémoire's work plunges us into a universe organized by a cool, cerebral guiding intelligence to give the widest possible scope to its sense of play. Her books are suggestive of origami: complex constructions that often double back upon themselves, distinguished by sharp creases, precise rules, and rigorous logic, but also by elegance, wit, and a palpable delight in exploring the limits of what the materials can be made to do.

In *Public Reading*, we see this sense of play in its game-like adversarial form, progressing as it does through a series of nested narrators who each strive to exert control over the text in a way that frequently smacks of one-up-manship. In the original French of the book's title, the reading is followed by a *débat*, a word whose meaning falls somewhere between *debate*, *Q&A*, and *discussion*, and which is closely allied to words for conflict and struggle, of which there is no shortage in the book, and which are no less real for being retroactively nullified. Aside from the conflict already mentioned between successive speakers, there are constant tussles between the speakers and their audiences, which are filled with active reader-listeners who stubbornly refuse to be cowed by any intellectual bloviating and who think they have every right to offer unsolicited advice, demand changes to the text, propose alternative interpretations, and point out mistakes. And they do have every right, unquestionably, even if not all the speakers are willing to acknowledge it.

Subtler, but more important, are the struggles for dominance on the level of language itself, most notably between its spoken and written forms, whose constant attempts to outmaneuver each other amount to a kind of Cold War running throughout the book, with regular outbreaks of fighting via proxies: the audience members who argue that the written text they have in front of them ought to overrule the version just spoken aloud by the author, for example. These proxies are constantly switching allegiances, however, sometimes in mid-sentence. Mémoire's characters entertain us by shifting back and forth, often clumsily, between high-toned, pompous, literary language and everyday speech. Effectively capturing these shifts in register was perhaps the biggest challenge of translating the book. It quickly became apparent that using a neutral, generic, "translationese" English for the casual dialogue would blunt (and therefore vitiate) its humor. As if that weren't bad enough, it would also do the characters a disservice by sanding off their most lifelike linguistic edges: people may write in this neutral dialect, may sometimes even straighten their ties, clear their throats, and make an effort to speak in it for a while, but they almost never chat, swear, or heckle in it. My choice at these moments was either to make the characters American or to make them artificial. I made them American. This decision—an audacious one for any translator—was rendered infinitely easier by the approval of Danielle Mémoire herself, who shepherded this translation through its last two drafts and consulted with me by email on points large and small for the better part of a year. She not only endorsed Americanizing the dialogue and wordplay, but often reserved her warmest approbation for my most Yankeefied expressions, such as *bozo* and *windbag*. For this, and for all her invaluable assistance, I am deeply indebted and grateful to her. There is no doubt the translation would not have been half so good without her, and I would like to think that, at its best, it provides the novel with one more origami fold, one more *débat*, this time a friendly one between French and English. I can think of no greater honor than to count myself one of the book's engaged, meddling, active readers. May it find many, many more.

Public Reading
Followed by Discussion

— Sometime today would be nice! We've been waiting here for ages now, and . . .

— Could you repeat that?

— What?

— What you just said. Repeat it.

— I asked you whether . . .

— I'm not asking you what you asked me, I'm asking you to repeat what you said. I'd be extremely grateful, moreover, if, before the words you're about to repeat—provided, of course, you consent to repeat them—you'd be so very kind as to . . . No, never mind, I can just as easily take care of it myself. And I will take care of it myself: Begin quote.

— What do you mean?

— The quotation. I mean I'm beginning it. That it has begun. I'm declaring it to have begun. Could you repeat that, please?

— I'm declaring it . . .

— What *you* said, repeat what *you* said. That sometime today would be nice. That you've been waiting here for ages now (ages, really!). And how much longer am I going to stay *stationed here like a potted plant*—stationed here like a potted plant, to my mind, suggests a standing person rather than a seated one. That would've been all I needed, to be left here standing up! Incidentally, I wouldn't say *stationed* in regard to a potted plant, I'd say *set*—set here like a potted plant, staring you down (speaking of which, have you not noticed my great difficulty in staring anybody down? It's because of my strabismus. The divergent variety. And stare down whom? Certainly not you, sir. The audience as a whole?), between my water pitcher and my bouquet of lilacs. End quote—No! One more moment, please. I have to thank the friend who sent me these lilacs. Thank you for the lilacs. Thank you very much indeed. End quote.

— And now?

— Now, what?

— And now, what are you waiting for?

— Now, I'm waiting for your questions. Your objections: I'm also waiting for those. Shouldn't we open the discussion?

— What? You're not going to continue?

— No. I'm finished.

— Finished? But that's not possible, you couldn't be finished . . .

— Yes, yes, I could be, I assure you.

— And you shouldn't be finished. You're here to read a work in progress, either in its entirety or as fragments.

— In its entirety. I have no other fragments.

— In that case, why did you agree to come? You should have declined.

— Because I thought I did have a work in progress. I thought so when I accepted the invitation, and it seemed to me I had plenty of time. When I realized it wasn't going to go any further than this, I tried to cancel: I phoned. No one picked up.

— You could have written.

— But, as you've seen, writing is a problem for me.

— And you gave up after—how many lines was that?

— I don't know. They're not written down.

— What are you talking about? Not written down?

— I gave up *before* those few lines, which I didn't write down. I improvised them.

— So you have no work in progress?

— Those few lines, which I improvised, are part of a work in progress which, for the time being, goes no further. I'm sorry. End quote.

— Ha, ha, very funny. Now what else are you going to read us?

— Read? Nothing: I haven't brought anything. I can improvise, if you like.

(*This really isn't what the audience would like, but they didn't come all this way just to turn around again and leave so soon.*)

— Fine, fine. Improvise.

— But surely you want to know the theme first. The theme is as follows: a public reading. It's an open-air performance, given early in the morning at the top of a tower. The reader is a man. Stately and plump, he appears at the stairhead, bearing a bowl of lather on which a mirror and a razor lie crossed. A yellow dressing-gown, ungirdled, is sustained gently behind him on the mild morning air. He holds the bowl aloft and intones:

— *Introibo ad altare Dei.*

Then, halted, he peers down the dark winding stairs and calls out coarsely:

— Come up. Come up, you fearful jesuit. End quote.

— Come up, Kinch. Come up, you fearful jesuit.

— Excuse me?

— I said: "Come up, *Kinch* . . ." You forgot Kinch.

— I didn't forget him, I omitted him. I also omitted Buck Mulligan. Why didn't you correct Buck Mulligan?

— I couldn't be sure. And then again, you did say you'd be improvising. "Stately and plump": I had my suspicions, but I couldn't be sure.

— Fairly strong suspicions, I would think. "Stately and plump": those are two words you don't expect to find together.

— You don't, except in a single case.

— Except in Buck Mulligan's case.

— Apart from Buck Mulligan's case, one would presumably be either stately or plump, is that it?

— With the understanding that one might be neither, yes, that's it. That's precisely it.

— A bird, for example, a baby bird fallen from the nest; if it's plump, which is entirely possible, it will, for that very reason, be non-stately.

— Almost for that very reason. Though, plump or otherwise, if it's young enough there's every likelihood of its not being the least bit stately.

— Or a dog, say. A big hunting dog. A pointer. Even a pointer on the stout side can be stately . . .

— To be truly stately, it would be better if it weren't.

— Let's suppose it is, though. Let's suppose the dog, though a trifle stout to the eye of a trained expert, which neither of us claims to be . . .

— I'll stop you there: I *am* an expert. Dogs are my specialty.

— We're supposing they aren't. This dog, which is stout, but almost imperceptibly so (and that, again, only to the eye of an expert, which you are), to the layman's eye . . .

— No, I'm sorry, there is simply no way. That it could be stately despite being stout, if that's what you were going to say . . . *Was* that what you were going to say?

— Yes.

— I cannot agree.

— Perhaps you'd rather take a different example. A woman? Would you rather take a woman?

— As an example? Yes. As an example, I'd rather take a woman.

— Then let's take a woman as our example. A stout
woman who is also stately. Literature teems with them.
Or *does* literature teem with them?

— Literature does teem with them, particularly in
the eighteenth century.

— Particularly in the eighteenth century, then, literature teaches us that a stout woman can also be stately . . .

— What in God's name are they going on about?

— We're just warming up. End quote.

(*The large hall—it is in a large hall that this short reading
has been taking place—the large hall begins to empty.*)

PUBLIC READER
(*a man*)
You're not going to stay? You're not going to ask any
questions? Is there to be no discussion?

SOMEONE IN THE AUDIENCE
Ask them yourself, since you seem so good at it.

SOMEONE ELSE
We've had enough. We're leaving.

PUBLIC READER
I beg you, no, stay, stay. That was just one of the many
works in progress I've brought. I'll read you another
you'll like better. Stay, stay.

(*They stay. The public reader pulls another sheet of paper from his hat.*)

PUBLIC READER

Begin quote.
(End quote.)

— That's all?

— That's all I've written, yes. It's a work in progress. It still needs an ending.

— What's going to happen next?

— Next, you're going to ask me questions. I'm going to try and answer them.

— I meant in the text.

— In the text, too.

— At this point in the text, the point where you left off, doesn't the public reader read something else?

— Yes, he does read something else: another text, a short story. Then he ends the quotation, people ask him questions, and he tries to answer them.

— This story he reads, have you written it yet?

— I would have read it, if I had.

— But you are going write it.

— Sooner or later, yes, I hope so.

— Couldn't you start with that?

— He arrives, he reads the story, and only then do they ask him questions?

— He doesn't arrive. He doesn't read the story. You

write the story. You go home, write it, and, if it really means that much to you, you can come back later and read it to us. The story, that is. You can spare us the rest.

— That's not at all what I had in mind. But I'm prepared to try. I *will* try. End quote.

— And that's the place where he reads the story?

— The place?

— The place in the text.

— There is no more text. It's very short. It ends there.

— You invited us here just to read us that?

— Ah, you didn't enjoy it.

— We enjoyed it, we enjoyed it. Only, as you said, it was very short.

— I have something else, if you like. It's also short. A poem. Do you want to hear it?

(*One can see by the look in their eyes that they do want to hear it.*)

— Ladies and gentlemen,

(*spoken standing up*)

In the beginning was the Word.
Those times have long since passed away.
In the beginning, so I've heard,
The grass was greener than today.

(*The room erupts into thunderous applause. The speaker ends the quotation.*)

— There's no denying it, that was a beautiful poem.

— About which, perhaps, you'd like to ask me a few questions?

— About the poem, no. About another passage.

— Please.

— In that charming little dramatic interlude, why do you say, "a man"?

— Because it's a dramatic interlude, complete with stage directions.

— Why do the directions say, "a man"?

— Because it is a man.

— But we can see that.

— What do you mean, you can see that? Me, you can see me! But I'm not the reader of the text.

— To be fair, though, you are the one who read it.

— I read it in the real world, not in the text. Didn't you understand that someone *within the text* was reading?

— Yes, of course. But I thought that person was you.

— . . . and that there were multiple readers within the text?

— Multiple readers? No, I didn't catch that.

(*The reader, in an aside*)

— You bend over backward for them, and this is the thanks you get.

(*Aloud, to the audience*)

— End quote.

— At the risk of sounding stupid, I have to admit that the business about multiple readers went right over my head, too.

— There are multiple readers, and at the same time only one. At the end of each section, there *will have been* multiple readers, but there's always only one reader who's just finished giving a reading.

— Aha! That clears it up. I feel much better now.

— You also had a very good excuse: you don't have the text in front of you.

— The person in the text, the one you just had interrupt you . . .

— Had interrupt the public reader . . .

— That person has the same excuse: they don't have the text in front of them, either.

— You're right. I'll have to amend that. The person *will* have the text. "Here, here is the text," the reader will say to them. Does that ring any bells?

— No. Should it?

— "Here, here is the text." That doesn't remind you of anything?

— No. I'm not as well read as you are.

— "Here, here is the text, quoth he." Funny, I'm sure that reminds me of something or other.

— But you don't know what?

— No. End quote.

— And *you* don't know, either?

— What those words remind me of? I was hoping you'd ask. Those words remind me of a song. "Here, here is the text": "Here, lady, here are my gloves, quoth he . . ." No? Nothing? You don't know it?

(*Nearly everyone in the room does know it, and they convey this information clearly and unambiguously through a variety of means, but the public reader, intent on displaying his beauteous voice, feigns ignorance.*)

— Oh, what a pity! Such a delightful song! I simply must sing it for you!

(*He sings:*)

In the merry month of May when the blooms blow free,
In the merry month of May when the blooms blow free,
When the blooms blow free, my bright beauty,
When the blooms blow free so beautifully.

Then the king's son travels far, over hill and lea . . .

With the fairest of the blooms his gloves fills he . . .

Which he offers to his jo on bended knee . . .

Here, lady, here are my gloves, quoth he . . .

You shall wear them on four days of the year only . . .

All Saints', Easter, Christmas, and St. John's jubilee . . .

(*Sustained applause.*)

End quote.

— And it ends there? Because, to be frank, I'd really prefer that you stop: I found you decidedly dull, madam.
    — I often am. I've also been told . . .
    — Wait: *madam*? It's a woman now?
    — It is I, sir. I am a woman.

(*With infinite grace, she draws two closing quotation marks
in the air.*)

— Questions?
    — Yes, I have one: you quoted, without attribution . . .

— By employing this gambit, which of course is not infallible, I had hoped to elicit a minor question, a question of little importance, but one that would, or so I thought, prove diverting for all of you. It's just that I'm not especially eager, you see, to enter into a discussion. I manifest, in order to engage in a discussion, in order to enable myself to successfully engage in a discussion, either too combative or too docile a nature, depending on the circumstances. I am endowed with a dual nature. Do you wish to talk about my nature? About me?

— No, God forbid!

(*There is, in fact, one person in the hall who says Yes, but unfortunately for us—we would then have had all the psychological detail, or at least all the biographical detail, we could have wished—he speaks too softly to be heard.*)

— I didn't think so, either.

(He means, "I didn't think you'd wish to (that you'd wish for us to talk about me)," which should, by the way, be fairly apparent to anyone who goes back a few lines and rereads, an obligation which it is evident that, in practice, nearly every (private) reader invariably prefers to avoid.)

— I didn't think so, either.

(*He doesn't repeat this: I'm the one repeating it, for the benefit of the private reader who's forgotten that it was just said (was just said by the public reader (that he has just said, "I didn't think so, either.")).*)

— I didn't think so, either (*said, once and only once, the public reader*), nor did I wish it. (*Meaning he didn't think others wished to, nor did he wish others to wish to. I think that's clear enough.*) Nor do I wish to engage in a discussion, nor talk about myself. (This, at any rate, is clear.) But I was thinking that, perhaps, since we have so much time left over, and since I've read everything I brought to read, I might start the text over again from the beginning (*he means, of course, start the reading of the text over again: to start the writing of it over again in the manner he's about to describe would grossly exceed the (approximately) one hundred and twenty pages to which he was, thank God, asked to limit himself*) and (*start reading the text over from the beginning, and*), for any passages still obscure to you (*for any passages of the text, the reading of which he's offering to start over again from the beginning, which remain obscure to the members of the audience*), explain them (*the passages, to the audience*) as we come to them.

— Yes, what a wonderful idea!

— Good. Off we go, then. Begin quote.

(*End quote.*)

— There's one thing that bothers me: you were invited here to give a reading from a work in progress . . .

— A reading to be followed by a discussion . . .

— Right. So you show up, you read, and the work in progress just happens to be the story of a guy . . .

— It's not a guy, I've told you: it's several; sometimes it's a woman; it's not a story at all; and I haven't read, I've improvised.

— Then you don't have a work in progress? And you were so set on putting in an appearance that you felt you were under an obligation . . .

— I was under no obligation I did not willingly impose upon myself. Works in progress I have in spades. I don't wish to read them in public. I have so little wish to make public appearances that I do not make them and did not show up. End quote.

— He didn't show up? How's that?

— She. It's a woman

— Begging your pardon, but I have the text here in front of me. There's no feminine "e" on the past participles. It's a man.

— I'm glad you didn't say, "What? But you did show up!" That's something, at least.

— You're not him, or her, we all got the picture, you hammered that one home well enough. If he didn't show up, though . . .

— She. It's a woman. I'll have to see about amending the text.

— If she didn't show up, who's she talking to?

— She's not talking, she's writing. And besides, the text I read you . . .

— Which you claimed to be improvising . . .

— He was improvising it. Or she. Or, more accurately, was pretending to improvise it. Or, more accurately still, had the reader he or she was depicting improvise it. As for the author—a woman—she stayed at home to write a book inspired by a situation which she, for various reasons she could elaborate, preferred not to experience firsthand.

— Namely?

— I said *she* could elaborate them: they're her reasons, not mine. Anyway, as you can see for yourself, I did show up. End quote.

— You're not going to read any more of it?

— Read? I didn't read: I improvised.

— You did tell me earlier you'd be improvising.

— And did you believe me?

— I believe you now.

— You clearly saw I didn't have a text.

— You were, it's true, walking along with your hands in your pockets. I must explain to the audience how I met you on the street.

— Explain it to them. They'll be tickled.

— Well, I was walking down the street . . .

— Rue Daguerre. Our paths didn't cross in opposite directions, however: I, hands in pockets, was walking ahead of you; you spotted me, quickened your pace, and caught up with me.

— We continued on our common course together.

— We were two men of letters strolling together down Rue Daguerre.

— We got on the metro together.

— We were heading for the same destination.

— You were on your way to give this reading.

— This reading that isn't one. You were on your way to listen to me.

— To listen to you and participate in a discussion with you.

— I, however, had no desire to participate in a discussion.

— You had no desire to read, either. Besides, you didn't have a text.

— You asked me if I wasn't worried: I was, and wanted to be.

— "Otherwise, what's the point?" you said to me. But, you said, if worse came to worst, you could always talk about your dogs. You could tell the story of your dogs . . .

— Of my dogs? But I don't have any dogs. We meet so often on Rue Daguerre, and have you ever once seen me with a dog? Let alone several?

— That's just what I thought at the time: "His dogs? But he doesn't have any!" I do know you have a cat.

— Tobermory.

— I ran into you one day on Rue Daguerre. You were searching for him. You seemed downcast.

— "Downcast" is an understatement: I was in despair.

— By the way, did you ever find him? (Please forgive my not asking sooner.)

— I did, thank you. And only then was I downcast.

— Downcast, despite having found him?

— Downcast *because* I had found him.

— You would have preferred not to?

— I preferred him in his unfound state.

— Is this what you intended to talk about in coming here?

— I don't believe so, no, it's not what I intended to talk about. And it's certainly not a story about dogs. It's not the story of a cat, either. It's the story of mankind. End quote.

(*During the span of time, however brief, occupied by the reading, two large dogs—two pointers, one male and one female—have remained lying perfectly still at the feet of the reader, an old man.*)

A YOUNG WOMAN
Rest assured, sir, I'm not going to say, "But you can't deny you have dogs!"

OLD MAN
No, miss, I can see you won't.

YOUNG WOMAN
You do, however, have someone say to the reader, in the text you read . . .

OLD MAN

I wasn't reading, miss, I was improvising.

YOUNG WOMAN

You improvise well, sir. But the fact is, you mentioned a story: the story was about dogs, and you have these dogs. Could you tell us the story?

OLD MAN

It's a very long story, miss. And from so long ago, and so sad . . .

YOUNG WOMAN

I'd love to hear a sad story. But as for long ago—it couldn't have been all that long ago: your dogs are still young.

OLD MAN

That's because the story isn't about these dogs, it's about their ancestors; it's also about my youth.

YOUNG WOMAN

In that case, yes: it must go back a ways. Are you sure you won't tell it?

OLD MAN

No, no, I will.

(*He tells it.*)

End quote.

— It goes without saying that you don't want to hold a discussion.

— A discussion, no.

— You didn't want to read, either.

— Nevertheless, I did: I didn't improvise, I read.

— I could have sworn you were improvising. And also to come here, you said you didn't want to come here.

— It wasn't I who said that, it was the reader. But it's true I didn't want to.

— Can you tell us why?

— Why I put that in the mouth of a reader?

— Why you didn't want to.

— Well now, what I'm going to say is something of a commonplace. And an inaccurate one, to boot; I hope you will accept it nonetheless (from falsehood, anything follows). It's a commonplace to say that writing is a solitary act. Solitude turns a man into a bear. And is it now, after I've been transformed into a bear, that I should appear before the public? What were you hoping to see? A bear?

(*He stands—he is a man: the feminine word-endings sprinkled throughout the text were merely a pathetic attempt to fictionalize him—walks out from behind the table, and, on reaching the front of the dais, executes a ponderous dance step of heartrending clumsiness.*)

— Mumma, Mumma (*he says*), dusky pearl that from out the sea of life I had gathered, in that sea have I lost thee once again?

— That was . . . something else.

— Actually, it wasn't something else, it was the bear. It was Atta Troll, the bear from Heinrich Heine. Which means you got a bit of literature after all. You can't complain. End quote.

— What's the story with that?

— It wasn't a story: his getting up and dancing doesn't constitute a story, or, if it does, only an extremely short one. Atta Troll isn't a story, either, but rather . . .

(*The audience—as at nearly all public readings, it is composed primarily of people of letters—is, naturally, familiar with the work:*)

— We know, we know.

— There is, however, a story I've tried repeatedly to write without ever succeeding to my satisfaction, in which *Atta Troll* plays a part.

— You wanted to write a story with a bear? How charming!

— With *Atta Troll*, the book. The protagonist, a young man I called Tancred, comes across this book—a very small book, in a handsome turn-of-the-century edition I own myself—which, together with a famous line from the great Corneille, inspired the whole story. As he's leaving the shop (the very one I visited), the young man meets a

girl, Aline, who dies a short time later, but not before he
falls madly in love with her. He subsequently becomes a
painter, an abstract painter. Many of his paintings, many
series of his paintings, will be entitled *Atta Troll.*

— That's not a story.

— Not even if it begins when Tancred becomes a
painter? With Tancred's paintings and the title *Atta Troll?*
Or, say, after Tancred's death, when the paintings are all
that remain? Not even if we watch as someone else—an
heir, a critic, a biographer—finally arrives, after patient
research, at the paintings, at the title *Atta Troll,* at the
day long ago—a lifetime ago—when Tancred bought
the book, when he walked out of the shop, when he met
Aline, when he *saw* Aline?

— Ah! Yes, in that case, it is a story. But a hackneyed
one. And anyway, this business about working all the
way back to that day, how could anyone manage to do
it? He might easily find the book in the personal library
of this . . . What did you say his name was?

— Tancred.

— Of this Tancred, and make the connection, of
course, between the book and the paintings, but as for
connecting the book to Aline, how could he possibly
manage to do it?

— How could *she* manage to do it: in my mind, it's
a woman. She couldn't. Which is why I didn't write the
story, I suppose.

— And I think I should remind you, furthermore,
that you didn't come here this evening to tell us the stories you couldn't write . . .

— But to read from a work in progress. Which is what I have done. End quote.

(*Three large pointers, two males and one female, lie at the reader's feet. He's known for never going anywhere without his dogs, and no one would ever dream of questioning him on what is generally accepted as a piece of harmless eccentricity.*)

— *Aline and Tancred*, that's the work in progress?

— No, I never had any intention of writing *Aline and Tancred*. I could tell you that my work in progress is that in which I talk about how I'm unable to write *Aline and Tancred*, a hackneyed story, it's true, but one that bears on the task of seeing, the pain of seeing, the complex network of meanings woven by desire and absence, but this wouldn't be any closer to the truth: in fact, I improvised that last section, the idea for which came to me as I was quoting from *Atta Troll*. Many years ago, I bought that book in the handsome edition I still have to this day. On leaving the shop, I saw this girl—all of a sudden, there she was, it was she. And that's how it always is with me: suddenly she's there, in my dreams, it is she.

— Are you going to tell us about your life now?

— No, no, I'm improvising. And it's someone else's life.

— But a life which, ultimately, you plan to write?

— As I said, it can't be done: working all the way back to that day, it's a thing that simply can't be done.

— What if it were Tancred himself?

— Tancred?

— Remembering it.

— I don't like memories, I like deductions. And Tancred's dead. End quote.

— You don't have any dogs?

— No.

— But you do have a cat?

— I do, madam. Robermory.

— That you lost and found again?

— I found it again, yes. In a manner of speaking.

— In a manner of speaking? What do you mean?

— Ah, madam, it's a long story.

— But, as it happens, we have a good deal of time left over. The text you read . . . *Did* you read it?

— Why yes, certainly. Hadn't you noticed?

— What I meant was: you weren't improvising?

— Do you think I can improvise for as long as that? Without once losing the thread?

— Actually, it seemed to me you did lose the thread quite a bit. But by no means do I want to debate the point, nor do I think anyone here wants to discuss or debate any point whatever. Since, however, we do have some time left over, as I said, perhaps you'd like to tell

us about your cat? The story of your cat, how you lost
it and found it again?

— Found it again, in a manner of speaking.
Unfortunately, no, I can't. You see, it's a true story and
I didn't write it. I don't write true stories. And I'm a
terrible improviser. On the other hand, though it's not
entirely finished, I could read you the story of the dogs,
part of which I was able to write, owing to the fact that
I don't own any dogs.

— Very well, if you like.

(*He takes a paper from the trunk he's known for never going
anywhere without, on the subject of which no one would
ever dream of questioning him, and begins to read:*)

— I was young, and there was a woman. A beautiful woman, and one who made quite an impression on
me.

I found myself, almost by accident, at a dinner party
she was hosting at her apartment, a Paris pied-à-terre she
rarely used. A foreign woman. She kept dogs. Pointers.

She was somewhat indisposed that evening. A nasty
fall had condemned her to weeks of inactivity. In consequence, I saw her as she received her guests on a chaise
longue, half-sitting, half-reclining. Wasn't all this too
much for her? Wasn't it . . . ? No, she said. Her only
concern was the dogs, walking the dogs, trying to think
whom she could entrust with the task. In New York,
where she lived much of the time, it was a regular pro-
fession, dog walking, but here? She would find someone

eventually, no doubt, but whom? And would she be able to rely on this person?

A lamp was lighted behind her. She was wearing a blouse, yellow, presumably silk; ever so slightly translucent, this silk, because of the lamp, because of the backlighting.

Her shoulder in the silken translucence, the flesh of her shoulder—or a bit above the shoulder, closer to her neck (though nearer the shoulder than the neck). Indented, softly creased by a fine strap, the flesh between shoulder and neck. I could not say: this line, this curve not found on younger women—was it that she was no longer young, had lost her youth, was it that poignancy? I don't believe I had any sensation of *poignancy*, any sense of *the* poignant, but I felt this emotion, yes, this welling up—I must, I think, say of love, but not love for a woman: for a few centimeters, for a few mere centimeters of flesh, for this groove, this imperceptible furrow in the flesh, I said: "As far as the dogs go, don't look any further. I'll take them out, if you like. I'll come by and take them out." She asked: "But twice a day? Every day, twice a day?" I said yes: "Yes, certainly. Twice a day, every day." I said that I loved dogs, that I'd be delighted to have dogs to walk, especially big dogs like hers. And I had nothing against them, certainly, though I've always preferred cats.

After that? After that, I came every day, twice a day, and walked the dogs. Upon my return in the mornings, I often joined her for coffee. At all events, she was a charming woman. A marvelous woman, and droll, wonderfully droll: I was constantly laughing. And on several occasions, in the evening, she invited me to stay for dinner. As a rule, I was not the only guest. She was a socialite, and well-liked.

My role? My role was walking the dogs. She felt no especial gratitude toward me: she would have undoubtedly found someone else in my absence.

And the impression I made? A poor one indeed. I was merely some nephew-or-other belonging to some friends-or-other. A pretty boy with no distinguishing traits. Not overly tiresome, not overly stupid (he laughs at the right moments), but not so wildly entertaining, either. And far too young.

No hope at all, then, you might say. Except, actually, hope—I tell you this idiotic story: the delicate strap, the flesh of her shoulder, the nearly imperceptible indentation, the flood of emotion—I, too, thought it idiotic the day after. Or rather, the day after, no. No, I was still an idiot the day after; I understood nothing, in my drunkenness, the day after: I was drunk. But *two* days after. Ah! Two days after, I no longer understood anything at all. A mature, brilliant woman, a woman who was, true, stunningly beautiful, or, better yet, who had been, once. And aloof, and imperious beneath her well-bred conviviality, and who appeared to see me no more than she saw, for that matter, anyone else, which was some balm to my pride. But, then again, had she seen me . . . Well, I had no more need of hope. I would have fled in horror, had I so much as glimpsed this hope. And I had the dogs on my hands. I believe we'll end the quotation.

— No, no: go on, go on. We're into it now.

— But *I'm* not into it. And I really don't want to go on.

— A little later, perhaps?

— Or another day. End quote.

— Your cat's not called Tobermory, then?

— I am not so literary as that, sir. Besides, it's not my cat.

— Oh? Don't you have any cats?

— I have one, sir. But not that one.

— And what's yours called?

— Tibert. Tibert Maury. End quote.

— I'd like to say something in regard to Atta Troll.

— There's nothing to be said in regard to *Atta Troll:* it could just as easily have been a different book—or no book at all, for that matter, but something else entirely. The key thing is the shift in perspective according to time, in desire according to perspective, and the perspective of desire, which is a desire for perspective, the continual anticipation of the same moment, symbolized by some ordinary object: repetitively, *liturgically* Aline, in her actualization before Tancred . . . And I've given up on writing *Aline and Tancred.*

— I meant Atta Troll the bear. I wasn't thinking of *Aline and Tancred* but of the public reader, when he plays the bear. When he dances like a bear. What would have made sense, to my mind, is if you had actually danced. Or sung.

— Sung?

— Earlier on: "In the merry month of May . . .

— . . . when the blooms blow free, my bright beauty, (*he sings*) when the blooms blow free so beautifully." Or if I had appeared at the stairhead, bearing a bowl of lather on which a mirror and a razor lay crossed?

— You couldn't have. There aren't any stairs.

— So I noticed. End quote.

— Or if you hadn't come at all.

— Pardon?

— Somewhere in the text—it is a text, isn't it?

— I should say it is!

— Somewhere in the text, there's the woman who decides not to come and read . . .

— A woman? Are you sure it isn't a man? Or several people?

— What matters to me is her, or his, refusal.

— Or theirs.

— It's the fact of not going. That's the point I'd like to discuss.

— Discuss away, discuss away . . . I myself did come

to the reading. Why do you suppose I came? Was it because, in my ursine solitude, I must have been starved for discussion? I discuss, I discuss, there's no end to the discussions I carry on with myself. I multiply myself in my objections, my opposing arguments, my opposing camps. I hardly know anymore which *me* I am, or even *whether* I am. If I accepted your invitation, however onerous it might have been for me in other respects (not least because I had no text and was forced to dash this one off in a hurry so as not to disappoint your expectations, though, as I can plainly see, I have disappointed you in spite of it all; I was very much afraid of disappointing you, and I don't like to disappoint: I find there's—ahem, well, anyway), if I accepted your invitation, it was in order to appear before you as one individual man, in order . . .

— So you're telling us the discussion is off?

— Why, we could chat instead, couldn't we, like regular people? Maybe I could relate a few folksy anecdotes about my childhood. Instead of some obscure genesis running itself ragged in myriad false starts, from dismal particular to barren universal, all rehearsed before your eyes and ears, I might have had an actual childhood, like a regular person.

— This seems important to you.

— It's just that, you see, I'd consider it a great favor. You'd like to do me a favor, wouldn't you?

— Of course, of course.

— Thank you for that. End quote.

— But he doesn't do it!

— What? What doesn't he do?

— His childhood, he doesn't talk about it.

— He talks about it, he talks about it. Only, this is a work in progress, and I haven't written that part yet.

— But you will write it?

— Certainly. It's central to my thesis.

— What thesis?

— Don't worry, it will appear in the text. All in good time.

— You'll talk about where you were born, and who your parents were, and that sort of thing?

— Where *he* was born, and who *his* parents were. No, madam. I was thinking more of minor details, as I said: everyday anecdotes.

— The kind, no doubt, that get told and retold within a family?

— And in the process construct it as a discursive entity, which is to say, construct it?

— Oh, I don't know about that. Maybe. What were you thinking of?

— What was I thinking of just now? I was thinking of the phrase "Often, but a little at a time, like poor old Swann." But that's not what I was talking about.

— No?

— No, not really. End quote.

— Anecdotes! Anecdotes!

— You don't want any discussion or debate, then?

— Why, don't you realize how long you've been debating with yourself? How you've multiplied yourself into so many opposing camps?

— And yet I simplified considerably.

— What we'd like is for you to appear before us as one individual man, to chat with us like a regular person, to tell us about your childhood, relate anecdotes from your childhood, the way regular people do.

— A tall order, I'm afraid. Then again, maybe—yes, there is that song, the one I didn't sing.

— I believe we were discussing anecdotes.

— It comes with an anecdote attached, and here it is: Now, my parents once had a very dear friend with whom they later lost touch, and who has since died, and I hadn't seen this friend since childhood (since my childhood). His name was Sami, short for Samuel. Sami Morgenrot. In the song I quoted, at the part where the king's son takes his gloves filled with flowers and offers them to "his jo" (*"sa mie"*) on bended knee, I heard— and, to tell the truth, I think I still hear—that he offers them to "Sami" on bended knee.

It never crossed my mind that this might be— as ample evidence had already shown me sometimes occurred, for example in "I want my friend Pierre, the one who is in jail," *"mon ami Pierrot,"* or "I have hired a shepherd lad, shepherdess Nanette. I have hired a shepherd lad, shepherdess Nanon," not to mention in countless poems ("Now go, said he, to your Sylvie / Again to

pine and weep / She shall you love your whole life long
/ For daring disturb my sleep")—a simple case of a common given name being used as a free-floating signifier,
which is a fascinating issue in itself, or fascinating to
me, anyhow; perhaps the specific reason it never crossed
my mind was that I'd never encountered, anywhere in
my experience of life, neither in songs nor in books, the
possibility of someone's being named *Sami*, such that . . .
This seems not to interest you.

— No, not at all.

— It doesn't seem so at all?

— It doesn't interest us at all. And, as for the quotation, you can end it right here.

— Ending the quotation, yes, that's just it. There's a
question I've been asking myself . . .

— There were none I asked *myself.* Luckily, friends
will always look out for you. From one friend who looks
out for me, to whom I sent a version of this text in many
respects very different from the one I've just read to you,
I received the following letter, which I'll also read to
you. It will prove enlightening, just wait and see. Begin
quote.

Paris, March 12, 1993 (*You wouldn't think so, but it
took me a good long while to get where I am today.*)

Paris, March 12, 1993

My dear Robert,

Here is the text, which (needless to say, as I've corrected a few errors in it), I've read, and now return to you, and on the subject of which there are a few elucidations I'd be most grateful if you'd furnish me.

I am correct in thinking, am I not, that this is the text you conceived on the occasion of that public reading you declined (*yes, the very same, though, as you've seen, as far as the reading was concerned, I changed my mind; I changed my mind without informing Robert (my friend's name is Robert, like mine), which is why he isn't here with us tonight*). It comes as no surprise to me, blah blah blah (*enthusiastic praise for the development of my work as a whole, which modesty prevents me from repeating*).

Yet, for all that, I did perceive one problem, namely (*here we go*) that of the quotation marks. You start off, you open the quotation marks (*the version I sent to Robert did, in fact, begin with quotation marks, with a pair of opening double quotation marks; I didn't say "begin quote," I simply typed the quotation marks, just like that, simple as you please; Robert's right, it was a mistake on my part*), then an initial dialogue follows, at the conclusion of which you close the quotation marks, a discussion begins—without any quotation marks being opened, because, within the world of the text, this part is not a text but rather the subsequent discussion, a discussion that will, however, be brought to a close by a pair of quotation marks: that was the text, which is followed by a discussion without any fresh quotation marks being opened, because, etc. (*yes*, etc., *you understood perfectly, Robert*). You use (*that is, I formerly used: it's no longer true of the present version, as careful listening will have permitted you, if not to know for certain, at least to suspect*), you use (*you used*) the quotation marks something like a multiplicative factor in an equation, which is distributed to the entirety of the text: opened once, therefore, they can be closed repeatedly. It's a lovely conceit (*thank you, Robert*); unfortunately, Robert (*"thank you, Robert" was me speaking to my friend, "unfortunately, Robert" was my friend speaking to me*), unfortunately, Robert, this raises a problem. When reading to oneself, one sees, as a reader, the quotation marks opening one single time only to close again and again: one understands the architecture of the text (*the architecture, Robert (I'm speaking to my friend now), the architecture, let's not get carried away, now!*) and I'm sure you'll tell me the text ought never to be read aloud, that it's out of the question (*that it was out of the question, Robert (I'm speaking to my friend), that it was*); but have you considered, Robert (*this is my friend speaking to me*), that within the text, the text comprising the text followed by the discussions, this text (*he means the text comprising the text followed by the discussions*), this text (*yes, that's definitely what he means*) will, at the moment preceding each new discussion, have been read aloud? It will not have had to address, in multiple instances, the eyes of successive individual readers, who would be able to see, as I did, the *written* quotation marks, but rather the ears, in a single instance, of multiple listeners. (*I'll open one last parenthesis here, within which, since after all it isn't* his *prose you came here tonight, some of you from quite far away, in order to hear, I'll slap the good Robert upside the letter, which runs on for pages and pages, with a set of closing quotation marks that will knock him into next week: close the quotation marks of Robert's letter, and close the parenthesis, too.*)

Robert was speaking to you of verisimilitude, not of reality. Robert didn't know that in reality I would be giving a reading of this text: he thought I was going to publish it (I will publish it). Had he known, he might have trusted to my remarkable abilities of expression and to the inexhaustible panoply of faces he knows only too well that I have at my command (this face here, and this, and this, and also this, but pay no attention to them now, please: I'm quoting myself—these are physical quotations—and now I'm moving on) to make abundantly clear to you, with the absorption of the current discussion and the public reader leading it, who came to life within it, into the fictional space defined by the next discussion, when the next discussion begins.

Robert was wrong, however, (and therefore right) insofar as what has just taken place—where we are, where you see me, with everything I know how to do, everything I'm able to do, and with everything that can be accomplished, for your pleasure and understanding, by both my presence and my person—is one thing, and a text, with its internal plausibility and internal consistency, is quite another. Well, as I said, this is a text—a book, even—I fully intend to publish: it will not always have me with it, nor will you always have me with you. Make the most of it. End quote.

— Questions?
   — Yes, I have one, sir.
   — I'm all ears.
   — This text, this work in progress . . .
   — It's not a work in progress.
   — No? It's finished?
   — Firstly, it is finished, it finishes right there. Secondly, it isn't one, it's several works in progress: in an extremely condensed form, and organized according to rigorous laws, topological laws in particular, it in fact represents the sum total of my works in progress. As you've noticed, it features multiple readers.
   — To be sure.
   — Each of these readers represents me in my capacity as author of each of these works. Speaking through any given one of them, I unfold for you the full theoretical, or possibly aesthetic, or sometimes ethical horizon of the respective work, of which he is sole author. Try me, and I'll prove it to you. See these trunks?

(*Shortly before the reading began, a number of large, cumbersome trunks had been carried onto the stage and left*

*there, where they might serve to arouse the audience's very
keen interest.)*

— Yes.

— These trunks contain—meaning *physically* contain, and, by the way, they're plenty heavy, believe me—
my works in progress, in their actual material form.
Therefore, on whatever subject you choose to question
me, provided it's one I've touched on in the distillation
I've just read to you (and I can hardly think of any I
haven't touched on), I'll be able to provide an answer
from the applicable work in progress: I need only open
the corresponding trunk.

— So there's a reader who's the author of the story
about . . .

— There is, there is . . . If the story exists, I can
embody its author, find its trunk, and unfold its horizon. But only if the story exists. *Aline and Tancred* does
not. It couldn't exist, and therefore doesn't. Had the
story existed, it would have been a hackneyed one.

— I wasn't referring to *Aline and Tancred.*

— Were you referring to the cat story? The cat
exists—up to a point, at least. It does not have, in its
existence, any horizon beyond that of the real world,
and it requires neither my trunks nor me.

— This condensed totality of your work . . .

— *In progress.*

— . . . Does it really talk about the cat?

— I see that a clarification is in order: this is the
condensed totality of my work in progress *and* of the
real world.

— Be that as it may, it's not the cat, or the cat story, that interests me. It's the dog story.

— Not a shaggy one, I hope.

— The story of the woman who kept dogs.

— Ah, you mean the story about the young man. The young man I once was.

— You're saying it's true? It's a true story?

— Though the story isn't true, and though there was neither woman nor dogs, I was no less once that young man.

— And how does it end?

— As you see me today. End quote.

(There are no trunks on the dais, hence the audience feels justified in interpreting the last few lines as nothing more than another of the reader's brilliant flights of fancy.)

— Could you tell us the ending of the story?

— Just like that? Off the cuff (the thing is, I haven't actually written it)? I don't know, but I'll try.

(This central section of the story, of which the extreme end, very much in the style of written rather than spoken language, will be read at a later date, should be told in a decidedly colloquial style. The reader will then break off, with or without giving a reason . . . Hang on, no, I've screwed something up. These are my notes I'm reading. Who the hell stuck these notes in the middle of my

text, anyway? And when I say the middle . . . Yup, sure enough, the rest is gone. Well that does it, we're pulling the plug. We're pulling the plug right now. Finito. Done. I'm outta here.

— You're not ending the quotation? Or closing the quotation marks?

— Those were in the text, those quotation marks. They're part of the text. No more text, no more quotation marks, no more nothing. Goodnight, folks.

— And the discussion?

— The discussion was also in the text (what morons!). In the text and in the title. Get it? And now, if you're really bent on having that discussion, I won't stand in your way. Go ahead, knock yourselves out.

(*He is outta here.*)

— You haven't left?

— What did I say! End quote.

— It doesn't exist, is that it, this story about the dogs? You haven't written that one, either?

— Written? Are you joking? I don't write anything, madam: I didn't write anything, I improvised.

— And you know how the story ends?

— I don't, but I can improvise an ending.

— And will you do it right now, on the spot?

— Certainly right now, on the spot. You remember how it began?

— Not very well, no.

— Sure you do: There's this young man . . . Suddenly, fleetingly, he falls in love with an older woman. In the heat of the moment, he offers to walk her dogs for her, three big dogs, pointers, two females and a male . . .

— Two males and a female.

— Whatever. This love vanishes almost as quickly as it arose, and, to quote his phrase, he still has the dogs on his hands. I believe that's where we left off.

— Then what?

— Right. Well, he shows up every morning. Every morning and every evening. The maid who answers the door hands him the leashes . . . Sometimes he catches a glimpse of her—THE woman—at the far end of the hallway, once she's up and walking around again with the help of her forearm crutches. She's almost always in her dressing gown: in the morning because she's a late riser, and in the evening because . . . well, reasons.

So she's usually in this dressing gown when he sees her, and it's in this gown we ought to picture her: the material is dark velvet. Dark crimson velvet, as Madame de Sévigné so charmingly says of certain families. Naturally, for her, Madame de Sévigné, this was a metonym. And it's a metonym for me, too.

From the end of the hallway, she (THE woman) calls

out to him, "Ta-ta!" or something in one of the many
languages she speaks fluently, which, as a rule, he doesn't
understand.

He comes back later with the dogs. She invites him
into the sitting room, or not. And he, for his part, sometimes declines her offer: he's glad to see her, of course,
(everyone is always glad to see her) but consider how
much time he's already lost to this chore! "To think,"
he'd say, "of all the time I've wasted on those damned
mutts!"

And again in the evenings: the maid, the leashes,
and—pardon me, but I'd like to go back to the dressing
gown. What I mean is, regarding this dressing gown:
there's the Sévigné-style metonymy, on the one hand,
and on the other, the likelihood that the woman is, or
that he imagines her to be, naked underneath. Not now,
of course—at this point in the story, he's not imagining
anything of the kind, but later, several weeks from now,
on the very last day, the departure day (the woman's
departure; she is never to return, as it happens), there will
be another brief—and, this time, indelible—moment.

— You're not going to go on?

— Go on? But I can't go on: I've finished. I've come
to the end, I told you: on the very last day. End quote.

— That was wonderful, marvelous. Bravo!

— And so theatrical!

— No: it may be wonderful, marvelous (bravo!), but theatrical, no. It is not theatrical.

— Not theatrical? What do you mean, not theatrical?

— That is to say, in one sense, if you insist, yes, OK, it is theatrical. It was conceived with theater in mind.

— Or maybe we should say instead it's theater-minded.

— Yes, you've hit the nail on the head: it's theater-minded. It has theater in mind, but it's not theater.

— It's not?

— No, and the proof is that nothing could ever be made of it as a theatrical piece.

— Really now, that remains to be seen.

— No, no, we can see it now. It's quite impossible. For instance, we already know that at the end of each discussion there's never more than one fellow who's been talking . . .

— One fellow, or one lady . . .

— Even worse!

(End quote.)

— It's a good point, though: why choose a form like this, given how complicated it is?

— Complicated? It's unusual, maybe, but complicated—it's not complicated.

— Unusual, then.

— What kind of answer would you prefer? A theory, or the truth?

— I like theories. A theory.

— There are theories galore, madam, in the text itself. You might have paid a little better attention. Were you daydreaming, or what?

— I was daydreaming, I was daydreaming.

(End quote.)

— That's exactly what I've been asking myself from the beginning: why a form like this?

— Do you find it complicated, or unusual?

— Unusual, mostly. But complicated, too, just the same.

— And don't you see what a good form it is? Good for a scattered and disorganized person like me? For example, I have notes, a staggering quantity of notes in a staggering quantity of notebooks, themselves packed away in a staggering quantity of trunks (I've brought just one of them with me, selected at random). I have notes on evil, on the question of evil. I deal with evil literally on a case-by-case basis, without ever managing to put them (the notes) into any coherent order; from time to time, I crack open a few trunks, I pull a few notes from a few notebooks, I put them in order (I can do so often, provided it's never more than a little at a time); this builds up a limited compendium of topics, sometimes a rich one, rich at least in poetry, like the story about the bird.

— What story about the bird?

— The one I read to you.

— You didn't read us any stories about birds.

— No? I could have sworn I did. The problem is that I have so many versions of this text. A bird figures in a good number of them. In others, to be sure, it's some other animal: a cat, dogs. Sometimes a woman. It really doesn't matter much, since whatever it is, it's never anything more than a device for approaching the question of evil from the standpoint of sensibility, which poses significant problems for me. Lord, do I have problems with sensibility! Practical problems, for one thing, because I'm an exceedingly sensitive individual: inordinately, unendurably, unbelievably so. I'm a perfect violin, I am, a perfect Stradivarius . . .

— We'd much rather have heard about the bird.

— And, for another thing, I have theoretical problems with sensibility, problems I'm clearly not framing well, because I've recently arrived at the following formula, which strikes me as rather unnerving: quote, sensibility is the a priori form of sensibility, (I might as well take advantage of the opportunity) end quote.

— Ladies and gentlemen, valued friends (*he has no friends in the audience, but he finds it helpful to imagine the contrary*), I am here to respond to your questions. You will ask them with all due care. As I've said, I am an extraordinarily sensitive individual. There are certain subjects you will avoid, so as to spare my sensibilities. You will avoid speaking of the bird: I cannot bear to hear the bird spoken of; the thought of the bird, of his tiny body, now stiffened, is a thing I cannot bear. You will not speak of Aline, whose remembrance haunts me. Nor of the woman with the dogs. You will not speak of the dogs. Do not speak to me of leprosy.

— Leprosy? What an idea! Why would we mention leprosy out of the blue?

— Rather *don't* mention it, as I've humbly implored you. My childhood reading about the lives of various saints impressed upon me the duty of tending to lepers. I aspired to sainthood. I aspire to it still. I hope to attain it by other means: the mere sight of lepers I cannot bear. Nor can I bear the thought of being unable to bear the sight.

— You *can* bear the thought, though. You ask us not to talk about it, but you're talking about it yourself, and you're bearing it.

— That is because I am, in reality, thinking of something else entirely. I speak and I speak, and I do not think of that which I say. I speak in order not to think, in order not to see of what I am speaking. I cannot bear to see it, nor to face the thought. I am not equipped to face the thought. Were I to face it, I should die.

(*He faces it. He dies. They bury him.*)

End quote.

— There was the story about the dogs with the ending we couldn't understand, there was the story you didn't tell about the cat, and now there's a story about a bird. What's the bird story?

— You know it already: it happened to you. One fine morning, you found a bird, a baby bird fallen out of the nest, adorably plump and pitiful, as your children had been, once. It was a swift. There it was, in the angle of your doorway, and if your cat didn't get it, it would soon starve. So you picked it up. You took a shoebox minus the lid, lined it with cotton wool, and made a new nest for the bird. You fed it bits of bread soaked in diluted milk. And, for all that, it died in a few hours anyway. Ah, that terrible moment when you held the tiny, stiffened body in your hands!

— You're right, that was unbearable."

— May I say something?

— Of course.

— You've finished?

— Of course.

— But you didn't say "End quote."

— No, I took care of it without saying. I did it by means of two little pen marks, which you couldn't hear. If you like, I'll repeat it.

— Did you hear them this time?

 — The quotation marks?

 — Yes.

 — Yes.

— Excuse me, I have a copy of the text here in front of me: there are no quotation marks.

 — What, no quotation marks? Just a moment, let me check: *that was unbearable . . . close quotes.* I can assure you, the quotation marks are there.

 — The next paragraph, I meant: "If you like, I'll repeat it."

 — I wouldn't like; don't repeat it."

— But you . . .

 — Indeed. It was a trap. His ears weren't as sharp as he claimed, I'd have sworn to that, and also to him falling right into my snare. Which he did.

 — Headfirst, you might say. And now you've got him. Just look at him struggle! He's flailing around like the devil.

 — You . . . you see him? You can actually see him?

 — Certainly: as clearly as I can see you.

 — Ah. If that's how it is . . . End quote.

— Mr. Robert Maury . . .

— No, you're mistaken: Robert Maury isn't me, it's my cat.

— Oh, I beg your pardon. I must have misheard your name.

— Albert. Albert Maury.

(End quote.)

— Are there any subjects, Mr. Albert Maury, you'd prefer we not broach?

— To spare my sensibilities, you mean? No, none. You allude, I think, to something that was merely a literary device, one I don't expect to retain in the final version of the text (aside from the fact that I used it inappropriately): do not speak to me of this, nor of that, nor the other. It's a fairly ham-handed method of introducing—or reintroducing, as the case may be—certain themes, either because I judged them indispensable and couldn't manage to work them in any other way, such as happens later on with Aline, or because, having dealt with them earlier in the text, I could find no better means of bringing them back, such as old Mr. Morgenrot.

— Sami Morgenrot?

— Sami was younger. The man we'd pass in the boulevards on Sundays, who would raise his hat and say, "What a glorious Sunday!"—each and every Sunday:

"What a glorious Sunday!"—that wasn't Sami, that was his father; that was the elder Mr. Morgenrot.

— You haven't mentioned him.

— No?

— No. You mentioned Sami and the song . . .

— *His* song: "Which he offers to *sa mie* on bended knee,

Which he offers to Sami on bended knee . . ."

(If they absolutely insist, the public may join in here:
On bended knee, my bright beauty,
On bended knee, so beautifully.)

— But you didn't mention his father.

— I didn't mention those laconic family legends, that secular liturgy, its significance at once quasi-cosmological and quasi-ontological? No? Nothing about that?

— I believe not.

— Nor how, through the connection I cannot help but draw between poor old Swann, "often, but a little at a time, like poor old Swann," and Mr. Morgenrot's glorious Sundays, I came to literature, to its heart, its structure?

— No, no.

— Well, as for that, I can't say I'm too surprised, since I've never managed to make much out of it.

— Furthermore, Aline, whom you cite as an example of a theme yet to appear . . .

— Don't tell me I've talked about Aline?

— You have.

— Do not speak to me of Aline.

(End quote.)

— Is he some kind of idiot?

— Who?

— Your reader.

— He's not my reader, he's myself. From time to time, I'll read my wife fragments of the text, one version or another of the text, in the course of which it sometimes happens, as it does here, that I get a little muddled. My wife will ask me questions and I'll write them down, along with my answers. That gives me one more fragment, another one too many. End quote.

— Say, you wouldn't by any chance have brought along something else, would you? Something short, that you could read quickly and we'd enjoy more?

— Why, yes, I do have something else, I have another text here. It's very different from the first, though organized around the same principle: There's a public reading, and it's followed by a discussion. Time and time again, the discussion is revealed to have been part of the text itself, and we enter into a new discussion, which is in turn revealed to have been part of the text itself.

— What's the difference?

— The content is very different. The reader is different, too.

— Reader? I thought in any event there would be multiple readers: we didn't pick up on it ourselves, but that's what you told us.

— There are multiple readers, and they are all one: I also said that.

— Though they're all only one reader at the start of each new discussion, they will have been multiple.

— They will have been in the sense that they might be men or women, young or old, sharp as tacks or dumb as rocks, but they're all variations of the same reader. In the other text, men or women, young or old, all are variations of another reader.

— Who isn't you?

— No more than the first was. Would you like to hear about this other reader?

— Frankly, no. One was enough.

— Suit yourself. End quote.

— I'd like to know . . .

— I'll answer your questions. But let me warn you, I'm going to be the other.

— The other?

— In contrast to myself and to the first reader, this other reader is a Roman Catholic. A Roman Catholic will be answering your questions, and therefore you'll take care that these questions don't exceed the ambit either of his abilities or his worldview, which is the view of faith. Try to confine yourself to God's justice. It's the only subject of any consequence, in his opinion.

— All right then: God's justice . . .

— What about God's justice?

— That's the question I'm raising. I'm raising the question of God's justice.

— God's justice isn't a question, it's an answer. It's the answer to mankind's suffering.

— Not at all: mankind's suffering is what calls God's justice into question.

— I see you're forgetting about the Redemption: all's well that ends well, there's the Redemption for you.

— But not everyone is redeemed.

— God alone knows the secrets of His mercy. And they were given fair warning, they can't say they weren't.

— But that an infinitely good God, who is also infinitely powerful, would leave men free . . .

— Just so, just so: He left them free. Would it have pleased you, personally, to be left otherwise? To be condemned to unremitting goodness?

— But free to be so evil? To such an abominable degree?

— Mysteriousness of His ways. And infinite richness of the world, from the highest degree of perfection to the lowest.

— Careful, now! That's Spinozism.

— Or Platonism: Catholicism is universal, it has a finger in every pie.

— I still insist, the evil committed . . .

— The evil committed: by which I understand committed materially, empirically, physically; as for intentions, they're a separate issue, one I'd subsume under that of individual liberty, which we've already covered—the amount of evil committed is strictly equivalent to the amount of evil suffered, which eternity indemnifies: undoubtedly, once at the right hand of God, once wallowing beatifically at the right hand of God, all will agree—and I don't just mean the martyrs, the willing volunteers, but also the unwilling, the doubly victimized, the sacrificed, the massacred, the tortured—that it was good man had been given free rein. And since we ourselves agree on this point, let us raise our voices in the following song of jubilation:

In the Lord I've placed my hope,
I trust His holy Wo-ord.

(*They raise their voices. End quote.*)

— I'd like to ask you a question.

— I'd like to ask you another. If you were in my place, would you have written "all will agree that it was good man had been given free rein," R-E-I-N, or "all will agree that it was good man had been given free reign," R-E-I-G-N?

— "All will agree that it was good man had been given free rein," R-E-I-N, I think.

— Nonetheless, you couldn't say man hadn't been given free rule, could you? Eh? Had you thought of that?

— No, in fact I hadn't.

— And you find that interesting, I hope.

— I do find it somewhat interesting.

— But it didn't cause your interest to peak?

— Pardon?

— I want to know whether your interest was made to peak. Whether you'd say, "Gee, that really peaked my interest!"

— No, it really didn't.

— Because you weren't especially interested. But if you had been, is that indeed what you'd have said?

— Maybe, sure.

— And you would have been wrong, because your interest would not have been made to peak, it would merely have been aroused, or piqued, P-I-Q-U-E-D. The proof is that when something has peaked, P-E-A-K-E-D, it has reached its apex and begun to decline, which is not your meaning here. Next time I give a public reading, it will be on topics such as these; I'll even toss in a few anecdotes from my childhood. You will, I think, enjoy it more, and the discussion will be livelier. In the meantime, end quote.

— Anecdotes and language . . .

— I will get to your question, madam. As a prelimi-
nary, however, I'd like to draw your attention to one particular fact: we are dealing here with a work in progress,
which I've read up to the point where I left off writing it;
therefore, the topics I find myself to have closed on will
in no way ultimately constitute the ending or conclusion, and cannot offer, to my mind, the special interest
these latter call for.

— You aren't especially interested in anecdotes or
language?

— In the question of anecdotes, in the question of
language. Not especially, no. Yourself?

— I'm moderately interested in language, enormously
interested in anecdotes. In the question of anecdotes,
not at all. I'm also interested in cats. An anecdote which
would interest me above all others is one about the cat,
but I seem to recall you saying you wouldn't be able to
tell it. Because it was true.

— A reader said that—I was speaking through
him—a reader you evidently misheard: he never said
he couldn't *tell* true stories: he tells them, believe me; at
times, in fact, people wish they could shut him up. The
thing about true stories is, he can't *write* them: he's like
me in that way.

— Which means you yourself would be entirely capa-
ble of telling us the cat story.

— I would be, yes. Unfortunately, I don't think I
have time tonight to prove it to you.

— Is it really all that long, the cat story?

— All that long, no, it's not all that long. Only, you see, there's the story of the cat, and then there's the story of the bird: the little bird I mentioned earlier, a robin. I found it one morning in the corner of my lattice gazebo. I called for Albert, my houseboy. The nest; the bread dipped in diluted milk; its eyes, so tiny and yet so intense; the soft palpitation of life and, a few hours later, the sudden stiffness of the cold little body—all that, I left to Albert, I left it all in Albert's hands. Now my conscience reproaches me. What if, just maybe, it hadn't been too late? I have a train to catch around ten, the 10:12, and there's still a chance I can make it, but I must be off. I am off. End quote.

— You're not leaving?

— Oh, for God's . . . The other reader's leaving; I myself am staying. Moreover, my poor dear sir, I've been alluding to this bird, the young bird fallen out of its nest, since the beginning of the text, since page—hang on, I'm checking—page 7. Do you really think I could have written everything from page 7 onward between this morning and tonight?

— You, no; the other, yes.

(End quote.)

— I couldn't be more thrilled, believe me, that in the end you decided to stay. It isn't you, however, who interests me, it's the other.

— The one who left?

— The one who didn't come; the woman who, as I'm sure you remember, stayed home to write the book.

— Naturally, I remember. I am the author, after all. That's another thing we mustn't forget. And it wasn't a woman, it was a man.

— You said earlier . . .

— Pure gallantry. Take my word for it, he's a man.

— This man, then . . .

— He was invited. He was to give a public reading, doubtless to be followed by a discussion. He didn't go.

— They were expecting him and he stood them up?

— They weren't expecting him, no. He cancelled, to be sure: he's not just a man, he's a gentleman. His thoroughgoing courtesy is one of the reasons he refused to appear: in his capacity as author—for he had been invited in his capacity as author—he was anything but courteous. He was a reprobate, in his capacity as author, a brute and a sex fiend, a deviant, a kind of monster (this is true of many authors). In his capacity as author—as long as he was within what he considered the domain of literature (irrespective, to be sure, of literary merit: his own works had relatively little), brutality, obsession, perversion, and monstrosity were all he knew; he recognized no law but that of syntax (his command of which, however, was not what he could have wished); he was not at all, in his capacity as author, the sort who could appear before a masked and civilized audience (every-thing civilized wears a mask).

— He wasn't alive to the contradiction? To the fact that he was this contradiction? He never thought of embracing it? Of making an appearance, *himself* cour-teous, civilized, and masked?

— That's what he did every day: every day of his life, as soon as he stepped out the door, he appeared as the courteous man he knew how to be. Moreover, why him? There were plenty of other authors for that, plenty of other men: for we all embody this contradiction, though each of us inclines a little more to one side or the other.

— So he stayed at home and wrote a book about the public reading he didn't give?

— It wasn't a book *about* the public reading, and cer-tainly not about the one he didn't give: it was a public reading, or rather many, since . . . well, it's complicated. And anyway, in the end—although without embodying anything remotely like the aforementioned contradic-tion—you won't believe it, but he went.

— He went?

— They begged and they pleaded. He said OK. End quote.

— I know you aren't him: besides, with you, it didn't take much pleading . . .

— Though people were hardly pleading with me, I

came anyway? Thank you for informing the audience.

— Though you weren't him, you still came, the same way he did.

— I didn't come *the same way* he did: I came without any pleading. Go on and say it: without any invitation.

(*He whistles for his dog and, dragging his trunk behind him, exits the hall in a huff without ending the quotation.*)

— Though I don't doubt that, in your case, it took a great deal of pleading . . .

— No, not so much. I was quite happy to come. For a variety of reasons.

— I have an inkling of one of them.

— Essential or trivial?

— *Essential* would be the word, I think. Yes, I'd call it essential.

— But I had trivial reasons, too. What's this essential reason you think you have an inkling of?

— By contrast, accepting after excessive pleading would, in my opinion, constitute a trivial reason.

— And one, furthermore, not numbering among my own. Come now, this reason?

— I'm proceeding, you understand, on the assumption, not that you are, but that you have many points in common with *the man who didn't go*—let's call him that; it will, of course, be a mere term of convenience, since, as we know, he did ultimately go.

— We could also call him by his name: Humbert Maury. Humbert Maury, the reprobate.

— The reprobate, *in his capacity as author.*

— In his capacity as author, it goes without saying. No stranger, in his capacity as author, to brutalities and perversions.

— The Man of the Night, as it were, in his capacity as author.

— Surely you're speaking metaphorically here.

— Metaphorically and metonymically. I was thinking of the dark side, the nocturnal side . . .

— And also, perhaps, of the fact that we typically dream at night?

— Literature being closely allied to dreams, yes.

— Literature, and art in general?

— Yes. The nocturnal side, by definition . . .

— If it can be defined . . .

— The nocturnal side can't show itself by the light of day.

— It reveals itself only in the nighttime of books?

— Yes.

— Or in the nighttime of art in general? The luminous nighttime of art in general?

— Yes.

— And in the nighttime of nighttime, too, of course, in our dreams?

— Yes.

— If you keep answering "yes" to everything I say, we really can't call this a discussion.

— There was hardly anything in the text you read that could be called a discussion.

— Do you have a problem with that?

— I do, a little, actually.

— You're attacking me, then?

— Attacking you . . .

— It's about time! End quote.

— That was interesting, that last ending. Not to mention educational.

— As one of my characters points out, however, for reasons of his own—because the whole text consists of nothing but characters, don't forget—we are dealing here with a work in progress, which I've read up to the point where I left off writing it; ergo, the topic on which it happens to close, in its last—but provisional—ending, not offering, in my view, the particular interest called for in an ending, deserves no more than any other topic to be the axis around which our discussion revolves: you might ask about any of the others and find me equally ready to respond.

— Yes, but what interests me, personally, is the last ending.

— The last but *provisional* ending.

— Obviously it's provisional: your interlocutor doesn't come to a conclusion.

— He's not my interlocutor, he's the reader's interlocutor.

— By "your" interlocutor I meant the one you were portraying.

— And, at any rate, it's not for him to come to a conclusion. I'm the one who will come to a conclusion, in my own good time.

— His remarks, the interlocutor doesn't come to the conclusion of his remarks. He said he had an inkling of something; he didn't say what.

— He didn't have time to say: the reader cut him off. What did he have an inkling of, do you think?

— That's just what I was going to ask you: what does he have an inkling of? What did he have an inkling of?

— Of nothing, in my opinion: the man's a windbag. With all his "nocturnal" horseshit he's managed to gain a few moments in the public eye. Why take that away from him? End quote.

(*Two large dogs, two pointers—one female and one male— lie at the reader's feet. Ever since the male, at the beginning of the reading, upset the vase of lilacs with its tail, they have remained perfectly still.*)

— No questions?

— It's just that your concluding statement was hardly of the type to encourage active debate.

— Let's not debate, then, let's just chat. Let's chat about language. For instance, we can talk about the curious word that is *still*.

— Still what?

— The curious word that is *still*.

— The curious word that is *still*? *Still*, as a word, isn't curious at all, at least no more so than any other.

— But I meant the curious word that is the abstract noun *still*—which differs, somehow, from *stillness*—as in the phrase, *the still of the night*, which the Littré dictionary cites from La Fontaine.

— The still of the night: in its tranquility . . .

— At a moment of pause . . .

— Like a single frame of film . . .

— The blue hour . . .

— *La vie en rose*. End quote.

— I'm mindful of the fact that I shouldn't dwell on the last, but provisional, ending . . .

— It isn't provisional. The piece is finished: *la vie en rose* is my conclusion. That's how it ends.

— And one dog's dead? Only two dogs are left. Or are they not the same dogs?

— As a matter of fact, no, they're not the same dogs.

— It's a different man, with different dogs?

— Different dogs, same man. The man from the story about the woman who had dogs.

— Did he keep the dogs?

— Those weren't the same ones originally mentioned, but yes, he kept them. He kept the original ones, and he kept their descendants. He became a dog breeder. You didn't get that?

— You didn't say it.

— She leaves, and she gives him the dogs.

— You said she left; you didn't say she gave him the dogs.

— "I'm giving them to you. Yes, yes, I insist you take them. They're such fine dogs, and so very fond of you." There it is, plain as day.

— You didn't read that passage. I'm sure of it. I was paying very close attention.

— "She was unpredictable, one might even say capricious: condemned to months of immobility . . ." did I read that?

— No.

— Dammit! This is infuriating.

— It's not so bad: you can read it now.

— Can I? (*He reads:*) She was unpredictable, one might even say capricious: condemned to months of immobility, her only anxiety, or so she said, was for the dogs; and now, all of a sudden, simply because she planned to travel by way of London, because she had been seized by a sudden urge to see London again: "I'm giving them to you. Yes, yes, I insist you take them. They're such fine dogs, and so very fond of you!"

They took up far too much room at my place in Paris. I held out for fifteen days before moving to the country. I live there still. End quote.

— And that's it? In short, all you can think to tell us is that he really did become a dog breeder?

— That *I* really did become a dog breeder, and how it came about. I'll also tell you more about the woman: how it was impossible to deny her anything. I, in any case, found it impossible, and I have reason to think I wasn't the only one; but then again I was particularly timid, particularly easy to wrong-foot; I've found myself in similar predicaments a number of times, though they were unquestionably less momentous and occurred at the hands of people who made much less of an impression on me.

The last day, the day before her departure—on that day I took the dogs out as usual. She wanted to keep them with her as long as she could: I was to pick them up the following day from the vacated apartment. And so I did. But on that day, the last day, when I returned from the evening walk—they say, I think rightly, that dogs can sense these things: her intention to leave without them—she opened the door to me; by then, she was walking with only one cane. One of the two males leaped up on her. Not in an aggressive way, no: in a surge of clumsy, puppyish affection the likes of which I'd never seen in him. Nor, in all probability, had she, as it was clear she hadn't been expecting anything of the sort. The impact knocked her off balance. I was close by and I caught her. I caught her by the elbow and the back, one of her elbows in one of my hands and my other hand behind her back. I can't say I took her in my arms, or held her in my arms. I was holding her up, but not holding her. With my hands, not my arms. She was *in* my hands. And she seemed so fragile there, in my hands.

She was a tall woman, or, at least—I was taller than she was, granted—at least she gave the *impression* of height. A haughty woman. Yes: and suddenly so fragile, so . . . defenseless. Something, too—perhaps it was the warmth of her body, her breath so near to me, the cry she uttered—not of fear, mind you, only surprise—there was something of the animal about her. Something doe-like. And those big dogs like a pack of hounds.

What next? Next, we laughed. She laughed, undoubtedly embarrassed—no one staggers, or totters, without feeling some degree of embarrassment—she broke into her beautiful, deep laugh, her magnificent laugh, which bore so little resemblance to her voice, though her voice was magnificent, too. No, I can assure you, this isn't . . . What I'm saying is entirely objective. I had always believed, even before, that she had the most beautiful female voice I'd ever heard. Her speaking voice, I mean (she didn't sing). And many people shared my opinion. I laughed then, too, I started laughing, out of politeness and sheer stupidity.

We have this word, *smitten*. It's usually applied to a first meeting, to love at first sight. Something sudden, like a thunderbolt, but, even more than that, something immediate. Whereas I—a woman, you understand, I'd known since childhood, since my childhood. Whom I'd seen every day, twice a day, for weeks, and the whole time—save for the emotion I've just described that evening with the dogs, that surge of feeling like a dog

leaping, like a clumsy, overgrown animal—I'd felt nothing
apart from fury at myself and my damned impulsiveness,
and regarded her with indifference, with boredom . . .
And I was to think back, ever after, during the intermi-
nable ever after of my life, on those days, on their light,
and on her, her gestures, the hand I'd brought to my
lips—her hand to my lips, the rings on her fingers—on
the light of those days of unsuspected happiness, right
up until the final moment of the final day: her metamorphosis into a doe, the thunderbolt I held in my
hands. E.Q.

— What does "E.Q." mean?

— End quote.

— Oh, I beg your pardon, I interrupted. What does
"E.Q." mean?

— It means I got tired of saying "End quote" and
abbreviated it to "E.Q.": E.Q.

— Since you've finished the dog story—you *have* finished the dog story, haven't you?

— As far as I'm concerned, yes.

— Since you've finished the dog story, now you can
finish the cat story. Or the Aline and Tancred story.

— *Aline and Tancred*, no: I can't. I haven't written it.

The stories I make up, I can't tell except in writing. I can tell you the cat story. If I tell it now, though, we won't be able to say we had a discussion.

— Did you want to have a discussion?

— God, no.

— Then you should be glad!

— I'm very glad. End quote.

— It seems to me you made things far too easy for yourself.

— Which is why that last ending won't be included in the text. It's exclusively for tonight's event: it's my way of letting you know that, in point of fact, I don't want to have a discussion. I was planning to tell you the cat story in order to avoid it.

— And this cat's name is Tibert?

— Tibert? No: you're confusing him with another cat, a literary cat. This is a real cat. He was, anyway.

— You never found him? Is he lost? Dead?

— I can't say I found him, nor can I say he's lost, and I sincerely hope he's not dead. Here are the facts: I had this cat, Buck Mulligan (that's his name). One morning, I find him gone: he's not in the apartment, not in the building. He doesn't normally venture out into the street, but hey, he has to be somewhere; I go down to the street—this is Rue Roger, where I live—and, sure enough, he was there, he had been there, people had seen him there around daybreak: a gray tabby, stately

and plump. And now? Ah, now . . . The fact was, there'd
been a battle, a cat battle, in which he would've gotten
the worst of it (he's like me: the peace-loving type), he
must be in the corner of some basement somewhere
dying, we'll never see hide nor hair of him again. But
suppose he *didn't* get the worst of it, suppose he beat
a seasonable retreat and got away unscathed? In that
case, what would have been his next move? He wouldn't
have taken Rue Froidevaux: there's always heavy traffic
on that road. He'd have headed toward Rue Daguerre.
Once on Rue Daguerre, Rue Gassendi, which also has a
lot of traffic, would be directly on his left. He wouldn't
have gone that way, he'd have turned right. I follow
suit and turn right, too, and what do I see, there on the
doorstep of a shop across the street, rolling around as if
basking in the sun, though there isn't any sun? A gray
tabby, momentarily hidden from my view by a pass-
ing van, during which time I say the following prayer:
"Please, God, let this be Buck Mulligan!"

I'm sure you all see why that's important: I don't say
"I hope this is Buck Mulligan" but "Please, God, let
this be him." By appealing to God, I'm requesting a
miracle, namely that this cat, if it isn't Buck Mulligan,
might become him through God's will; what I'm saying
(what I'm implying) is: "If this cat isn't Buck Mulligan,
please, God, let it become Buck Mulligan, *make* it Buck
Mulligan." And God did.

I crossed the street, I went up to the cat, I said—I
inquired—"Buck?" He leaped into my arms just the way
Buck, or any other cat that knew me, would have done.

He was Buck to a tee—same little scar on his nose, same tattoo on the inside of his ear (Ca 37 27)—with the single exception that he was a shade lighter, and, in that respect, possibly a shade handsomer. It was as if God had decided to cut a few corners and confine Himself to the essentials: scar, tattoo, friendliness, recognition of its name and my voice. Was I going to quibble with God over color?

I departed for the country. I left the cat behind in Paris, along with a note to my son, who hadn't returned home yet. I didn't tell him the full story: I hadn't given him a religious upbringing, and I didn't want him to catch me in a flagrant contradiction of what he took to be my settled beliefs. I told him, "Keep a close eye on Buck, he almost got himself lost again." We'd come close to losing him on several occasions (and, in effect, we had lost him). I also told my son, "If, as they say, cats have only nine lives, then Buck Mulligan must be nine cats." Truth will out: when it can't proclaim itself openly, it takes the path of exaggeration.

By the time I got back from the country, God had made an effort at remediation, and the cat was a little darker. A little *too* dark, in fact. Such is life. End quote.

— Are you finished? Are you finished reading?

— Yes, sir, not only reading, but writing: the text will be exactly as you've just heard it. Not one jot or tittle will be changed.

— Oh, I'm so disappointed!

— You'd have liked it to be longer? I quite understand.

— I don't know about longer. No, maybe not longer. Different. Just the slightest bit different. More importantly, I thought something was going to happen.

— So nothing happens, in your opinion? It's a little thin on plot for your taste? Is nothing good enough for you people?

— First of all, yes: to my mind, anyway, it is a little thin on plot. But that's not what I was referring to. I thought something was going to happen *outside of* the text. Because of Humbert Maury.

— Remind me again who Humbert Maury is. I wrote this, as usual, extremely hastily, and I wasn't paying particularly close attention.

— Humbert Maury, the reprobate: the one who was invited and didn't go.

— And yet he does go, in the end.

— Precisely. I was thinking that he, and you with him, would ultimately have decided to go *in his capacity as author*. As Man of the Night, as pervert and monster, before a masked and civilized audience . . .

— And that there'd be fireworks, is that it?

— Of some sort, yes, that's it.

— Which there weren't. End quote.

— It's apparent, nonetheless, that you've thought about this subject . . .

— I've thought about a lot of things. To which of my many thoughts do you allude?

— To our nocturnal side. I'm inclined to believe you've thought about it—I inferred as much from the preceding passages: "It was in my capacity as author I was invited, in my capacity as author they wanted to see me; I am not visible in my capacity as author; in my capacity as author, I am unpresentable. Therefore, I will not go." And also from the fact that you said: "What if I accepted anyway? What if I went and appeared in my capacity as author? As brute, as pervert, as monster?"

— And in the end, I would have given in?

— So it would seem.

— I, give in? End quote.

— Well, is something going to happen now? You're not giving in: does that mean now is the time when something will happen? Something truly brutal, perverted, and monstrous?

— Ah, but what if the text—I won't say this text, the one I've read, but any text—and I won't say *drained*, perhaps, but took upon itself the greater part of that which dwelt in the author—in any author, and in many a reader besides—of the nocturnal, the primitive (the perverse, the brutal, the monstrous), to such an extent that there remained for the author (for any author, and for many a reader besides) nothing, or nothing to speak of, he could manifest as such?

— As such?

— As nocturnal, as primitive. What if, just as writing finds no expression in him save through the nocturnal and the primitive, the nocturnal in him, the primitive, found no expression save through writing?

— Giving in, at that point, would mean nothing.

— Or not giving in. No, nothing at all.

— And nothing could possibly happen.

— Outside of the text. End quote.

(The tape deck continues to emit a few labored rasping noises; Robert Maury emerges from backstage; he wears a yellow coat, unbelted, somewhat resembling a dressing gown; visibly moved, he turns to face the audience.)

SOMEONE IN THE AUDIENCE

That really started to drag near the end there, and we couldn't make head or tail of it. Can you help us out a little?

ROBERT MAURY

Sadly, no, I cannot: I couldn't make head or tail of it myself, and my brother—my brother is the author—left instructions that were none too precise.

We won't have him here with us tonight, or any other night: as some of you are already aware, he went away with the intention never to return, and the fact of the matter is that he won't return. He wanted to tend to leprosy patients, an obsession which had held him in its thrall since his childhood. I tried to dissuade him, don't think I didn't. Don't think I didn't say to him: "Why you, Albert? You who have such talent, and whose thought could do so much for the leprosy of the soul, why, you, the leprosy of the body?" Don't believe for one moment, either, that I'm not eaten up by this regret: if only I had gone in his place, then he'd be here with you tonight, and, instead of my own voice, which, as it happens, is remarkably similar to his (people are always mistaking us for each other on the phone), it would be his voice you'd be listening to now. But I had a family to support, while he had only his cat and his dogs, and I could take the cat and the dogs.

The cat and the dogs are doing well, thank you, but I can't say the same for Albert: he has leprosy. As he was throughout his life, even so do we find him in his last letter: curious, yearning to understand—*and now*, he says *I know whereof I speak*—impervious to suffering—leprosy patients, for that matter, don't really suffer, as is well known—steadfast in the face of death—though people can survive for quite a long time with leprosy—and always more concerned for others' welfare than for his own, as you can see by what he says to me: *But as for you, Robert, be very careful of yourself, and take due precautions against the leprosy of the soul, which is more contagious still. Your loving brother, Albert.* End quote.

(*On the street*.*)

— How long has he been standing out there reading from those papers?

— A good two hours. He was already there when I left to drop off the kids at school, and I don't think he's taken any breathers: I went out again a bit later to run to the post office and he was still at it.

— Screaming like that the whole time?

— Less so early in the morning. He cranks up the volume a notch or two every time I go past.

— And what, there's no police officer around? No one to intervene, if only for the guy's own sake? They might be able to get him some help, poor bastard!

— And so young! End quote.

— Is . . .

— I cannot answer questions. I am not the author. Having failed, in view of the fire hazard it would pose to the building, to find the conditions satisfied under which he had insisted this event be staged, not only has he declined to read, a thing he never intended to do in the first place, but he has not come at all.

— What were the conditions?

— His conditions were as follows: Hidden from the audience's view by a low wall, a reader, presumably

---

* Rue Daguerre

myself, was to manipulate divers puppets, of which nothing would be seen but the shadows projected onto a larger wall by the light of a fire (you appreciate the problem). There were not to be so many puppets as entrances in the text (or exits, if you like, it all comes to the same thing), rather each puppet was to be reused in accordance with a pattern of succession it would have behooved the audience to bend its efforts toward accurately predicting. The author would have appeared afterward to elucidate the composition, and only then would there have been the discussion on which we had all pinned our hopes. And whose loss we shall bitterly regret. End quote.

— I'd like to revisit a passage from not too far back, which has been bothering me for several reasons. It's the cat, the story of the cat. Buck Mulligan.

— But he isn't called Buck Mulligan, as perhaps you already suspect, yes? Is that what's bothering you?

— No.

— No, you didn't suspect, or no, it doesn't bother you?

— Neither. I didn't suspect, and it doesn't bother me. What is he called?

— Sami. He's called Sami. Does that bother you?

— It makes no difference to me either way. What bothers me is your selfishness. You didn't spare a single thought for that cat, for the real cat, Buck Mulligan . . .

— Sami. He's called Sami.

— You didn't spare a thought for the real Sami, for

what might have happened to him. Whether he was lost, or living with another family, or dead in the back of a basement. Your concern wasn't that Sami should exist, but that he should exist for you, that you should have him. Otherwise, you wouldn't have said, "Please, God, let this be Sami,"—this cat here, the one I see in front of me, the one at hand, make it be him, so I can have him, and to hell with the other one, the real one.

— Did I ever say, "to hell with the other one, the real one"? Or that I didn't miss the other one, the real one, did I ever say that? I didn't say it: I miss him. Of course I miss him.

— But it wasn't Sami you were thinking of. Your prayer wasn't for him. You were only thinking about yourself. And, what's more, I don't believe God would have made a mistake.

— A mistake?

— On the color. God would not have made a mistake.

— Indeed, God doesn't make mistakes. God wasn't *mistaken* about the color. God wanted to demonstrate His power to me. He demonstrated it to me by performing a miracle—and it was a miracle—but He deliberately made it imperfect, because God judged me (I am in fact a great sinner, I am selfish, I was thinking not of Sami but myself in my prayer), God judged me unworthy of a more perfect miracle. This is the God in whom I place all my hopes for the real Sami: that, while He's at it, He'll protect him, alive or dead.

End quote.

— Which role in the preceding dialogue do you attribute to yourself, given that, as you've asserted (*nowhere, however, in the text now submitted for the private reader's consideration, has the public reader asserted anything of the kind; this might very well be a reference to an undocumented conversation, perhaps one taking place backstage before the event, or might even, owing to a momentary and understandable lapse in his attention, be due to an error on the speaker's part. The fact that the speaker has not asserted anywhere that such a thing happens, however, does not necessarily imply that such a thing doesn't happen*), it frequently happens in the course of these imaginary discussions that it is the speaker, rather than the reader— the public reader, that is—who acts as your mouthpiece.

— I don't occupy any of the roles in the preceding dialogue. Those were people I overheard on the train, and I was reporting what they said. I did it to pad out my time. End quote.

— Some texts are designed to educate, others to entertain; some share in our pain or give form to our anxieties, and thereby, in however small a measure, offer us solace; some make us unaccountably happy.

— That isn't a question.

— My question is this: is there any goal among these which the text whose reading you've inflicted on us tonight aims to accomplish?

— You're just asking me whether it aims, correct? You don't absolutely insist that it reach the goal? It aims at all of them.

— You meant it to be *educational?*

— While holding out scant hope that it would be, yes, absolutely. And it did educate me; it also entertained me a little, though not very much. There are pains in which it shares, gnawing anxieties to which it gives form.

— *This* text? Form?

— A very tenuous form, for a very short time.

— But surely there couldn't be anyone the text aims, even for a moment, to render happy?

— Unaccountably, you mean?

— Unaccountably especially.

— Not anyone, really? How can you be so sure?

— I don't know, but I am. Or will someone speak up and prove me wrong?

(A gleam of hope flickers in the public reader's eye: his friends are among the audience. But not a single hand goes up. He takes a notebook from his pocket.)

— What are you writing?

— Nothing, just a note about a work in progress. Another work in progress. In this work, we follow a character—in reality, me—through a traumatic recurring dream: it's nighttime, and he finds himself in a place he recognizes only from having been there countless times before in the same circumstances in the same

dream. He also knows, either from catching glimpses
of them or from somehow sensing their presence, that
other people are here, too, people who are his friends,
or at the very least his acquaintances (Thérèse Aubert,
Miss Trellis, Melchior Martigon, Messrs. Morgenrot the
elder and younger, Buck Mulligan, Aline, the Maury
brothers . . .). Something terrible awaits him in this
place, something the dream never divulges or reveals.
In this work in progress, we try to imagine—or he, the
hero, does, or I myself do—the possible nature of this
threat the dream is holding over us.

— And?

— And nothing. I told you: I'm just jotting down a
note. End quote.

— In your work in progress . . .

— This work, or the other one?

— You mean you really do have the other one?

— Yes, thank God.

— We see, in this work in progress . . .

— The other one?

— Yes, the other one. A few characters we saw in the
first work crop up again: Buck Mulligan, Aline . . .

— Charles Morgenrot . . . Indeed they do.

— Charles Morgenrot, is he the father?

— The man we'd pass in the boulevards on Sunday?
Who would raise his hat and say: "What a glorious

Sunday!"? Each and every Sunday: "What a glorious Sunday!"? I never knew his given name. There's no particular reason to suppose it was Charles. I was thinking of the son.

— The son? Sami?

— Ah, I made a mistake. It's because of Charles Swann: Sami reminds me of Swann, and Swann has always reminded me of Sami.

— How nice for you!

— Sami, physically, bore no resemblance to Swann. He was small and very dark, with an adorable monkey face. My mother used to say . . . Never mind. But he had this much in common with Swann: he was on a first-name basis with the great and the good of this world, including the king's son who presented him with a pair of gloves.

— There are also some characters we haven't seen before: Thérèse Aubert . . .

— We've seen her. She's the woman with the dogs.

— Didn't you say she was a foreigner?

— Yes, but she married a Frenchman years back.

— Melchior Martigon?

— Melchior Martigon, as it happens, is not in the text (in the one I've just read you). He's in the audience. End quote.

(*The aforementioned text which in this first part will undergo few modifications, will continue for a further, and approximately equal, length of time. It will be read in its entirety by a single performer, either male or female, who may, within reason, alter the pitch of his or her voice from low to high and high to low. The reader will have at his or her disposal assorted props, such as wigs, hats of various shapes and sizes, spectacles, monocles, pince-nez, canes (most notably forearm crutches), and a domino cloak with matching mask.*

A table will be placed center stage, which he or she will use in whatever ways the text and inspiration dictate (sitting behind it or on it; standing in front of, behind, or on top of it).

All of this will be long, tedious, and extremely beautiful, thanks in large part to the lighting effects. End quote.)

— Are you telling me he wrote this? That this is what he wrote?

— What he dictated to me, yes. Every day. A few lines every day.

— Would he read it over?

— I read it over to him.

— And what would he say?

— He wouldn't say anything. He would just keep going. He would just keep going.

(End quote.)

— One thing I noticed in this work in progress . . .

— In the other work in progress?

— In the other one, yes. You mention Aline by name, but you don't mention Tancred. Is it not the same Aline? Is it not the Aline from *Aline and Tancred*?

— The very same, madam. I omitted myself for the sake of discretion: I am Tancred.

— Tancred wasn't a painter?

— I also paint, in my spare time. Over and over again, I paint the rectangular frame with its horizontal bar—the transom—framing an empty space (empty except for adumbrations—in order to make it *that* space—of the curtain folds, the shadow of the lilacs, the clock face in the soft lamplight), such as Aline was never to see it . . . Nah, I'm pulling your leg: it's just something I made up, a licentious story. A terrible idea. End quote.

— Is *Tancred and Aline* the licentious story, the terrible idea?

— *Tancred and Aline* isn't the title, in any case. The title is *The Transom*. It is licentious, yes, and the idea is probably not the best. The terrible idea was to make use of it.

— Make use of it? You mean tell it?

— First to tell it, then to make use of it.

— I'm not following.

— I'll explain. You remember *the man who didn't go?*

— Humbert Maury, the reprobate.

— In real life, his name was Albert. He did finally end up going.

— And this man was you?

— He wasn't me, but I had him in mind. There's— this is what I said to myself as I thought about him— there's the brutality, the perversion, the nocturnal side of our nature, and, on top of that, and not unrelated to it, is the idea of writing as a perilous enterprise: I wouldn't claim, nor would he, that to write is to risk your life, but that you can put your heart and soul into your work and lose your mind in the process, that writing dumbfounds your reason, confounds it—the greater part of it—can, in a word, *half-founder* it, is something I believe as firmly as he does. That said, he gives a public reading. They think it's the author they're going to hear read: the man who writes. What a joke! Reading, you see, isn't perilous at all.

— But how does *Tancred and Aline* fit into all this?

— Suppose the author *is* Tancred. And all the licentious, and therefore compromising, things he says happened once upon a time to Tancred, in reality happened to him . . .

— And which, having written them, he goes and reads aloud, presenting them as his own experience?

— Which, having written them, he goes and reads aloud, presenting them as having happened *only to Tancred.* Literature, you see, although perilous and in many ways audacious, is at the same time woefully innocuous: whatever audacity it reveals can never be anything *but* literature. The text, however, once read to you and judged by you according to literary standards, hence neither good nor bad but hopelessly innocuous, if only then, without warning, and *outside of the text*—now diminished and simultaneously expanded in light of his presence, his flesh-and-blood being, his undeniable reality before your very eyes—if the author told you he was Tancred, if he said: *I am* Tancred . . .

— Yes? If he said that?

— Nothing. At any rate, I didn't tell the story, and the idea was a terrible one. In particular, the character choice was terrible (anybody could be Tancred). It would have been better to stick with Melchior Martigon.

— Melchior Martigon?

— The dirty old man. The horrible roué.

— But you said he was here in the audience . . .

— And am I not? End quote.

— The story, *Aline and Tancred* . . .

— The title is *The Transom*.

— What I think is, you wrote it, maybe you're even pretty pleased with it, but you thought it was too short to form the sum and substance of your reading all on its own; I think you've been struggling in vain from the very beginning to make up for its brevity—though anyone hearing your prose would count that as one of its chief virtues—through the ridiculous expedient of these amateur theatricals, and at a given moment you're going to *foist* that story on us.

— You mean later on in the text? But it's finished: end quote.

— Didn't you have any other works in progress you could have read to us instead of this one . . . ?

— All of them at once, instead of this one?

— Any of them, if you'd had any. They certainly couldn't have been worse. Didn't you have another one?

— No.

— What about your trunk? What's in the trunk?

(*In a corner of the stage, a heavy trunk is indeed visible.*)

— Through the expedient of this trunk, I was hoping to keep your curiosity piqued till the end of my reading. I have no further need of it now. As you can see for yourselves, (*he opens the trunk and turns it upside down*) it's quite empty. End quote.

— Is it really empty?

(*This question refers to the heavy trunk visible in one corner of the stage.*)

— That I don't know; it isn't mine. It was here when
I arrived. Maybe it was left behind by some other reader
who came here to read on some other evening.

— Don't you want to look inside?

— I'm not convinced that's something I can do.

— Sure you can, sure you can. I attend all of these
readings and I noticed it here a long time ago, more than
a year and a day. It doesn't belong to anyone anymore.

(*The reader looks inside the trunk.*)

— Well? What is it? What's inside?

— Papers.

— Pages? With writing?

— Pages with writing, yes. Lots of pages with writing.
End quote.

— And what he finds in the trunk is none other than
Aline and Tancred?

— *The Transom*. No, sir, it is not. What he finds in
the trunk are meditations, meditations I'd venture to call
philosophical, formulated though they are with no lack
of commendable humility, on the subject of happiness.
The paradoxes of happiness.

— Paradoxes?

— How to know, for example, whether, on finding the
practical conditions of what is at least relative happiness

assembled around you—relative, specifically, to another's misfortune—you should or should not endeavor to enjoy them.

— That depends on your capabilities. And it's not a paradox, it's simply a question. An *academic* question.

— Let's assume I have—let's assume this person is me—all the requisite capabilities.

— Well then, there you are! You're happy.

— The paradox—and this is only the start—the paradox arises from the other person. From the contemplation of the other person in his misfortune.

— Another person's misfortune makes you unhappy?

— I hate to blow my own horn on the subject, but yes; at least, I believe so—or, at least, I can't manage to disbelieve it. The question torments me.

— There's still no paradox, only a negative condition.

— A negative condition?

— You can't be happy in the face of another's misfortune: his lack of happiness renders your happiness incomplete.

— But the other person doesn't see it that way. "Why are you torturing yourself?" he says. "What more do you need?"

— What would he have you do? What would he do in your place?

— He claims that if he were in my place, he'd be *living it up*. He'd *count himself lucky*. And he goes on to say, "You *don't know* how lucky you are."

— If he's giving you his blessing, then go ahead: count yourself lucky.

— In *comparison* to him? I should let his misfortune, in effect—let the misfortune of some, including
him, furnish the happiness of others, including me? Yet
some third person, under conditions similar to those I
described earlier as defining the empty void within this
same happiness, this third person suffers.

— He manages to find cause for suffering? What
cause? Or is it the same one: another's misfortune?

— His own internal misfortune: the nocturnal, the
primitive, the infantile within himself. He suffers from
it so much it kills him.

— God rest his soul.

— But would I say he *didn't know* how lucky he was?

— Good question: would you?

— I wonder. End quote.

*(There is, in fact, a trunk onstage, but no one is showing
the slightest interest in it; if the reader—a woman—had
been counting on anything of the sort, her efforts have been
wasted.)*

— I was expecting a licentious story; that's why I stuck
around. You're not going to read it after all?

— Read it? No, sir, I haven't written it.

— So what you're telling us is, the story was true?

— Oh, sir!

— It's the true stories you can't write, you said so
yourself.

— *A reader* said so.

— Not this again!

— I haven't written it because I haven't had the time, though I have made several attempts at writing it in several different forms.

— Don't say you're going to read us several versions in several forms!

— I didn't bring them. If you want, I can summarize the story for you.

(*They do want. She complies.*)

— Tancred is a young painter, and he's in love with a girl, Aline.

He finds a patron in the form of Melchior Martigon, an old roué—a caricature of an old roué.

Melchior Martigon has stayed on good terms with one of his former mistresses, Thérèse.

They're both very attractive, Melchior and Thérèse, but, as I've said—I said it of Melchior, at least, and it's equally true of Thérèse—they're not as young as they used to be.

Aline and Tancred are also very attractive.

More so than Tancred's novice paintings (in which he does, nonetheless, detect signs of genuine talent), it's the young couple themselves who—like so many young couples before them—are the real object of Melchior and Thérèse's interest. In their customary fashion, they, he and Thérèse, plan to divvy up the spoils and then toss them aside afterward: Thérèse getting Tancred, Melchior getting Aline.

Melchior's potent charm, however, falls flat with Aline; not so with Tancred Thérèse's.

— Come again?

— She means it's all systems go with Tancred and Thérèse.

— Thank you, yes, that is what I mean.

Tancred, whose heart still belongs to Aline, doesn't fall in love with Thérèse, nothing like that, but she's driving him to the brink of madness.

— Does this go on for long?

— Oh, hardly more than a few days.

— I meant your story, does the story go on for long?

— No, it's almost over.

— And he gives in?

— Gives in?

— Tancred. To the old bat's charms.

— I wouldn't call her an "old bat." Thérèse is perhaps fifty, maybe less. They're very young.

— Aline and Tancred?

— Aline and Tancred, yes. And Tancred does give in, to be sure, but only once. The scene takes place at Thérèse's country house: he thinks Aline has been detained in Paris and will join him on Sunday. In reality, she's going to Melchior's. To his place, with him.

— She's been detained in Paris by Melchior?

— No. Unbeknownst, if not to Thérèse (who might well have been tipped off by Melchior), unbeknownst at least to Tancred, she's gone to Melchior's country house. Melchior and Thérèse are country neighbors.

— And there *she* gives in.

— Aline? She acts as if she might. But no sooner does she arrive at Melchior's than she gives him the slip, cuts across the fields to Thérèse's house, sneaks in unseen through the back door, and finds her way to the little side room where Thérèse keeps her dresses, which has a view into the bedroom (into Thérèse's bedroom, directly across from the bed). Aline is familiar with the house: in the past few months, she's spent a good deal of time there.

— Now, look, we thought this was almost over.

— It is over: There's a transom above the door of the little side room. Aline pushes a stepladder under this transom. She climbs the stepladder and waits.

— What's she waiting for?

— Didn't I say she was jealous and had her suspicions? She also had a weak heart: she looks, she sees, she dies.

— And it's over.

— Yes.

— What a dumb story.

— Exactly what I was afraid of. End quote.

— It is dumb, though, that's true enough.

— In point of fact, I haven't quite finished. The finished story is marginally less dumb.

— Well, finish up and then let's drop the subject.

— You need to ask me some questions. Questions get my juices flowing.

— We have no idea what to ask.

— Ask me what happens afterward.

— Afterward? Right afterward?

— Or long afterward: there's also something that happens long afterward. But right afterward: right afterward, Melchior arrives, either in search of Aline (who, you recall, ran off from his house), or because he was invited to dinner. He's told the news . . .

— Who tells him the news?

— Thérèse. Or Tancred.

— Do they themselves know the news, Tancred and Thérèse?

— They heard a crash nearby; they investigated; Aline was dead. They break the news of her death to Melchior.

— And where they were at the time, does anyone tell him that?

— They?

— Tancred and Thérèse.

— Melchior might know without being told, though Tancred doesn't suspect the truth.

— What truth doesn't Tancred suspect?

— That Melchior and Thérèse may be in cahoots. This is something Tancred won't suspect for many years. Even then, it will take someone else to plant the idea in his head.

— Is all this important?

— No, not so much.

— Skip it, then, skip it.

— I am skipping it, or rather I'm picking up where I left off: what a prospect of scandal this raised, ladies

and gentlemen! Luckily, Aline hadn't sustained any inju-
ries in her fall, because it had been broken by Thérèse's
dresses.

— She didn't die from the fall?

— She fell because she was dead. Melchior gathers
her up in his arms . . .

— Better late than never . . .

— He carries her to a nearby bed. On Sunday morning, they send for a doctor, one who won't try to com-
plicate matters with too many inconvenient questions:
the young woman arrived late the previous afternoon (it
had been late in the afternoon when she died), said she
wasn't feeling well, and went straight to bed.

— No one went to check on her?

— Does the doctor ask that question, you mean? He
does ask. He's told there wasn't anyone to go and check:
it was the servants' day off (that much was perfectly
true), Tancred spent the night at Melchior's (Tancred
did spend the night at Melchior's), and Thérèse turned
in early. Scandal averted.

— And long afterward?

— Fairly soon afterward, but permanently and forever, Tancred's painting style undergoes a change. With
the exception of one portrait of Aline, *Aline with Lilacs*,
owned by Thérèse, who defends it tooth and nail from
Tancred's intermediaries (he will never again see her
in person), he destroys all his early works. For the few
already sold, he contrives trades. From then on, he pro-
duces large-scale canvases just barely classifiable as fig-
urative (some put them squarely in the category of the

abstract). The vague human figures people sometimes think they discern in them are Thérèse's dresses.

— And *Atta Troll?*

— An in-joke: it's the name of my cat. He looks like a bear. End quote.

— It isn't all that bad, you know. It just really does drag on a bit too long.

— The short story, you mean?

— No. I'm not talking about the short story, which is deadwood and needs to be cut. I mean the whole thing: it drags on too long, and you should've thrown in a little more variety. Not in the text itself, however . . .

— No? The text is varied enough, in your opinion?

— Varied enough to lend itself to a completely different presentation, or should I say *representation.*

— Representation?

— Yes. Because there are simultaneously one and many readers . . .

— Aha! You think there ought to be multiple readers rather than only one. Rather than me.

— Rather than you, no question. But multiple, definitely not: one reader, in the text, takes on all the rest.

— He takes them on, you think?

— A single reader, then, but one furnished with an assortment of props . . .

— Such as spectacles, wigs, hats of various shapes and sizes, capes to make him stately and plump?

— And cats, and dogs . . . You've thought about this, apparently.

— Not about the cats and dogs, no, I admit I haven't. But as for the rest, I've got it right here in my trunk. I brought all of it here with me in my trunk. At the last minute, I decided to do without it.

— Bad call.

— Yes, I see that now, and I thank you for your input.

— That's what I'm here for. End quote.

— The short story

— I agree: I'll cut the short story.

— Cut it, no. Tighten it up is what you need to do.

— Tighten it up how?

— By putting it down on paper, for starters. Next, by reducing the number of characters to three: Aline, Tancred, and Thérèse. I can't see what purpose Melchior Martigon serves except schlepping the corpse, which is something Tancred could do. You don't seem terribly convinced. Are you that attached to Melchior Martigon?

— Attached, no. It's not that I'm attached to him.

— What, then?

— I thought I'd made it clear.

— I have no idea what you're talking about.

— Just look at me. End quote.

— He means *he's* Melchior Martigon?

— I am Melchior Martigon.

— Oh! I beg your pardon. I didn't know your name.

— Names, schmames . . . But did you come to this event not knowing who I was?

— I was in the neighborhood, I saw the lights on, it said "Free Admission" (subject to available seating), there was still plenty of available seating, I had nothing better to do, I came in, I listened.

— You weren't disappointed?

— Not at all, sir! You're a good reader.

— And now you'd like to ask me a question?

— I wanted to know about the robin.

— It wasn't a robin. I live in Paris, you see: I don't think there are any robins in Paris. I've never seen one, at any rate. It was a blackbird. For years now there've been massive numbers of blackbirds in Paris: they sit on your rooftop screeching their little heads off, they wake you up at the crack of dawn, they remind you of your small-town childhood.

I'll fill in a few more details for you: one day, while I was in the middle of writing this book, I found a blackbird, a tiny baby blackbird, adorably plump—the way human children can be, when they get enough to eat. That blackbird was the inspiration for the passages pertaining to it, as well as for the woman who narrates them: as you'll be able to see for yourselves, once the book is published, by verifying that all the adjectives and past participles have been changed (to the extent, of course, that they need to be) to their feminine forms, the person who talks about the blackbird is always a woman.

— She doesn't talk about a blackbird. She talks about a robin.

— Or a swift. My nostalgia can transform a blackbird into either a robin or a swift. Nostalgia, however, though a powerful emotion in its own right, pales beside compassion: I felt a truly unendurable compassion for the little blackbird, though the anticipatory thought of its tiny body cold and stiff in my hands was more unendurable still, and the idea made me balk. How I regret it now! Despite the bitter lessons of past attempts, I should not, indeed, have abandoned my efforts: with proper care I might have saved this one, I might have succeeded with this one where I had failed with so many before. In a matter of weeks, maybe days, he would've been perching on my shoulder, and I'd have taught him to whistle. You'd be hearing him now, this very moment, whistling "The Colonel Bogey March" for you. Instead of which, he's rotting under a thin layer of dirt.

Let's whistle. Let's all whistle "The Colonel Bogey March" together, in memory of the blackbird I didn't save.

(*They whistle.*)

— Or maybe "La Jeune Garde"? Would I have taught him to whistle "La Jeune Garde"? Let's whistle "La Jeune Garde" together in memory of the blackbird, and of dashed hopes.

(*But there are those in the audience who refuse, those who have never learned "La Jeune Garde," and those unable to*

whistle. Among the few who are ready, willing, and able,
some start at the "Prenez garde" line and others at "Nous
sommes la jeune garde." The result is an atrocious, though
feeble, cacophony, which depresses the public reader's spirits.
He ends the quotation.)

— I would like, with apologies in advance to my friends
here, as this is a point I don't think interested them in
the least (there was a lot of yawning in my vicinity), I'd
like it if you could expand on your ideas—you were
terribly confusing, as it turned out—regarding *the man
who didn't go.*

— "Humbert Maury, the reprobate." In real life,
his name was Albert. He wasn't a reprobate at all, and
he was among those for whom writing was a perilous
enterprise.

— So I gathered. Hence a public reading, the least
perilous enterprise in the world . . .

— In theory.

— A public reading seemed to him somehow at odds
with the act of writing. And he couldn't reconcile himself to it, to the reading, unless he could reclaim, by
some means or another, something of the act itself . . .

— Since the public imagined they were going to see
him *in his capacity as author*, and since, as he saw it, one
isn't an author except in the act itself.

— That his reason, however, would be dumbfounded,
should he give the reading, that it would be confounded,

half-foundered, or even less than half, was not something he could envision, naturally.

— Naturally.

— His reputation, on the other hand, not as an author but as a gentleman, in the hypothetical event that, after having read, he cast himself, with plausibility if not veracity, as a participant in the drama whose seamy underside he'd just exposed, his reputation as a gentleman might well have been foundered. By more than half.

— He would have lost by it, certainly. Thus, you can read or you can write, so long as you lose!

— But you didn't say that. You didn't do it, either.

— The reader, perhaps, does it in the text. There's no way of knowing. I haven't finished it.

— And what about you? Seeing as how you're the one who did come.

— Oh, but I'm not really an artist, you know. I'm not an author in the highest sense of the word: I write a little here and there, without ever risking either my reason or my life. In my case, there's no contradiction.

— Nothing's going to happen, then? Even though you came, nothing's going to happen?

— No, nothing. In fact, I'm about to leave. End quote.

— Much earlier in the text, you were talking about happiness. On the question of happiness . . .

— The question of happiness doesn't interest me. I'm interested in enjoyment, though I deplore the modern evolution of the term, which I use in its Spinozist sense, *fruitio*. I'm interested in the *fruitio existendi*, which, as I understand it, must necessarily be infinite.

— But one dialogue . . .

— I wasn't *discussing* happiness in that dialogue, but rather evoking the conversation: the presence of those who took part in it. It was in May. Not happiness, but those endless May evenings.

— Aren't you lyrical!

— I rhyme, as well, you'll note. And so, with that: end quote.

— Endless May evenings aren't a source of happiness for you?

— They're a source of pain. Likewise Fragonard.

— Fragonard?

— As I said. End quote.

— I'd like to ask you a question. It appeared in the text. You didn't answer it, as far as I can tell.

— Yes? What question is that?

— Why choose such a complicated form?

— I didn't choose it, it chose me. It's not remotely complicated, and it's not a form, it's a theme.

— No, it's a form.

— A theme. It has the effect of a form.

— I don't understand.

— I'll give you an example. I'll take a major one. I'll take as my example *One Thousand and One Nights*. You know the form of *One Thousand and One Nights*?

— Of course.

— Well now, it's not actually a form. The embedding of nested stories is a form in appearance only, on the surface only. In reality, it's a corollary of the main theme, or one of the main themes, which is salvation by storytelling. The main theme of salvation by storytelling engenders this nested form, which serves to illustrate it.

— Or vice versa.

— No. And the proof is that this theme recurs on various scales throughout the text, so far as it is a text.

— That might be a structural effect. A fractal form.

— But such is not the case. The theme is proliferative in and of itself. And it's the structure that is the effect.

— If you say so.

— I do say so.

— And what's *your* main theme?

— Salvation by storytelling. End quote.

— It gets all abstract toward the end there. I wasn't wild about that. I liked it better when you were talking about yourself, about concrete things with emotional weight: your cat, that little bird . . .

— I don't talk about myself in the text: it's a text.

I can't write about concrete things. I can't write about things that happen to me.

— You don't have a cat?

— No, no, I do have a cat.

— But you didn't lose it and find it again?

— I found it, yes. In a manner of speaking.

— So it was all true?

— That depends on what you mean by "true." It's not true, for instance, that the cat's name is Sami. Its name isn't Buck Mulligan, either.

— What is its name?

— I could tell you, but it would be a lie. Also, the events didn't take place on Rue Daguerre. I thought "Rue Daguerre" had a nice ring to it, like something out of a book. I had to carry out a few inversions, displacements, and condensations, as I always feel compelled to do when I write. It's funny, but as far as writing is concerned, I'm incapable of telling it like it is. I try, mind you, it's not that I don't try. But it's no use: I have to invert, displace, condense. I have to translate. What can I say? That's just how it works.

— But you can when you talk? Tell it like it is, I mean: you can do that when you're talking out loud?

— Or at least like it seems to me, yes, speaking aloud, I can.

— So, with this cat, couldn't you tell it like it was, talking to us out loud?

— Like it seemed to me it was? Yes, I could. End quote.

— You lost your cat?

— Yes.

— And found him again?

— If you can call it that, yes, I found him again.

— And yet you told the story in writing. You were hardly risking your reputation as a gentleman, only as an author (by the by, I found your allusions to public exposure, in the seventeenth-century sense, altogether idiotic . . .

— Far-fetched, I'll grant you, but idiotic, certainly not! Who's closing this parenthesis, you or I?

— I am:)

— And the quotation?

— The quotation, too.

— It's a fair point, though: if you lost your cat and then found it again . . . *Did* you lose it and find it again?

— In a manner of speaking, yes.

— Yet you also wrote the story: you read it to us.

— The way I wrote and read it wasn't the way it happened; I inverted, displaced, condensed, and translated.

— But you could tell us the story as it really happened, speaking aloud?

— Yes, I think I could. I wouldn't start at the very beginning, though: I didn't change much about the beginning. I'd start with me leaving for the country, which is where I began my translations; next, I'd jump back in time to the portion of the story I didn't witness firsthand.

— Then by all means, do.

— I am, I am. Here it is: I was going to meet my wife. I'd left my son a note. In this note, I told him the cat was nine cats. I could write this all the more easily for knowing it wasn't true.

Upon arriving in the country, I told my wife about the miracle and about the cat being lighter in color. I told her God had restored our cat to us, but only *in a manner of speaking*. She said, "If it was only in a manner of speaking, God didn't restore him, He gave him to us. And it isn't *our* cat. Speak for yourself, if you've decided to adopt him. As for me, I've never even laid eyes on him." (My wife is known for splitting hairs.)

We got back to Paris, and the first words out of my wife's mouth were, "Lighter? What do you mean, lighter? If anything, he's darker." My wife has an extraordinary eye for color and nuance, as do I, and her remark astonished me because the cat was *not* darker. He was the exact color of our cat. In fact, the cat *was* our cat: I must have been the victim of an optical illusion the day before (having to do with the sunlight, perhaps, or the absence of sunlight; I have my own pet theory on the subject), which my wife thought she could turn to good advantage by using it to play along with my miracle, whereas really it was an entirely different miracle of her own.

Psychologically speaking, the hardest thing for my wife to endure is the knowledge that, through her excessive precautions, she's awakened suspicions that would otherwise have remained dormant. I would've been perfectly happy with things as they were. I would've had my cat, my cat in a manner of speaking (as I would have continued to believe). But now, no: something wasn't right. A few weeks later, my wife, with tears in her voice, finally came clean.

To backtrack a little: I'd phoned my wife in the country. I'd told her the cat was missing, he wasn't in the apartment, wasn't in the building, someone had seen him on Rue Albert Maury, but he wasn't there, either. "Not to worry, though," I'd said. "I'm going back out to check the other streets: he might be roaming the neighborhood, happy as a clam, while we're tearing our hair out. OK, I'm off." With that, I'd hung up. "Well now," she'd thought to herself (she said), "Buck (my wife calls me Buck: I'm on the plump side and she finds me stately), Buck's gone looking for him and won't find him, because he's right: the cat's out roaming the neighborhood. While Buck's searching Rue Martigon, the cat will be lolling in the sun on Rue Morgenrot, and when Buck finally reaches Rue Morgenrot, the cat will have moved on further afield." She said that she said, "Dear God, if my cat is lolling in the sun on Rue Morgenrot at this moment, and if some passerby should see him, let that passerby who sees him be my husband, let it be Buck." And God granted her wish. You see me here before you, a bit plumper and less stately, she says, than the real Buck—may God protect him.

End quote.

— Can we return to happiness?

— No, miss, we cannot. It's in the nature of happiness that we cannot return to it. It is situated in time. It is under the aegis of time.

— What do you make of time regained?

— What do I make of it?

— Consider what you've just said: happiness is in time; happiness, according to you, doesn't return. Therefore, time doesn't return, either: no time regained.

— As for happiness, the fact is . . .

— Yes, yes. But, when you get right down to it, time is what interests me.

— It's all part of the same question, as I see it: there is no happiness but past happiness—as for present happiness, whether a happiness that is present or a present that is happy, I am, as I think you'll have noticed, a Kantian; I am virtuous and Kantian. There being no happiness but past happiness, happiness that is no more, in the quality of it's being no more, and probably even *because* it is no more, it is not, in fact, true to say that it does not return: it returns, and the time with it, in the aspect of its loss; it returns lost.

— It is only regained lost?

— Precisely. And do you think it's all fun and games? It's not fun and games, it's a source of pain. This pain is what I see in Fragonard: not beauty imparted, but beauty departed. In that which remains—the sky, the marbles, the light screening of trees: that which is no longer taking place, for which they served as setting. The luminous pain of Fragonard. Who is, along with Tancred, my favorite painter.

— But what do you know about Fragonard? What if he was a blithe spirit? What if he was joyful? Contented?

— Oh, joyful, contented . . . But I'm also joyful and contented. I need very little.

— And are you entirely sure Fragonard wasn't painting from life?

— I'm not at all sure, and it makes no difference to me.

— . . . That he wasn't painting what he saw, simply because he saw it? Taking pleasure in seeing it? Are you sure that what he sought, what he wanted to capture in his paintings, wasn't exactly *that* setting, *that* light, *that* day?

— And not the lost light? The light of a time *qua* lost?

— Yes.

— A person seeks one thing and finds another. What if he wanted to catch in the snares of his canvas the light of that particular day, that light, that day (I won't accent the words, if it's the same to you), before it was no more, and because it would be no more?

— Meaning something does, in fact, happen in the present?

— Loss. Loss is felt in the present.

— But if that which is regained, having been lost, is only regained *qua* lost, if it can't be regained except as lost, my question to you is: what good is it?

— Its value lies in the presence of its absence, in the enjoyment of its painful luster. I'll give you an example: I was in the country this morning (I live in the country; I came here by train). I was taking in this beautiful May day, its resplendent light. *This* beautiful day and *this* light. And it was the light of May days past, the absent presence of May days past. When the blooms blew free. And the king's son traveled far over hill and lea.

End quote.

— And the bird?

— I should have avoided that subject. It is, for me, a source of shame and regret.

— Because you did nothing to save it?

— On the contrary, I did everything I could. In doing so, I had to neglect this text, which is why it's so bad. But anyway, the owl—it's a barn owl, an owlet; it moves with the grace of a cat; I gave it a cat's name, Tobermory—this owlet survived. I brought it with me. You'll see it, but not until later; it's still sleeping backstage. It spreads its wings only with the falling of the dusk. In the meantime, ask me some questions.

— Very well. What sort of questions?

— Oh, about my regrets, for example, or—this is the same example—about the world's cruelty.

— Gladly: the world's cruelty.

— We cannot conceive of it. Not only can we not conceive of it, we cannot think about it except in the aggregate, and the aggregate is far less—this is paradoxical, in a sense, but true—the aggregate is far less painful than the individual instance. The proximate instance, anyway, far more than the distant aggregate: the little owlet in the angle of my doorway far more than the millions of people I've never seen.

— We can at least think rationally about aggregates and numbers.

— And we can also think rationally about the fact that what we're thinking about is emotionally affecting, without actually *being* emotionally affected.

— Obviously: intellect and rationality take over the reins from emotion and sensibility.

— In the process, they repress the knowledge of *which* emotion is involved. And if they repress it to that extent, what's to prevent me from repressing it even further: no mercy, every man for himself, *vae victis?*

(*The owl, at this moment, would emerge from backstage. To the immense delight of the audience, it would fly around the hall, where the lights would have been dimmed at the public reader's request for the greater comfort of this nocturnal bird, and would sustain its flight for the duration of the text, which, as ill luck would have it, finishes here: end quote.*)

— May I say something about the very end? Or is it not really the end?

— You may in either case. But it is the end.

— I hate it.

— Is it the world's cruelty you're thinking of?

— I'm not a big fan of the world's cruelty, but I meant the owl.

— You don't like owls?

— It *would* emerge from backstage, it *would* fly around the hall . . .

— Perhaps you would have preferred it to fly for real, right here and now? Have you ever had an owl in your house? Do you have any idea what kind of mess it leaves behind? It's best to know what you're talking about before opening your mouth.

— But that's not what I meant. I meant . . .

— Or maybe you don't believe I could have done it? First of all, I certainly could have: *it's entirely feasible*— there's nothing physically or humanly impossible about it—that I might save a barn owl, that I might tame it, that I might bring it with me into this hall, and that I might turn it loose in this hall, which it would then proceed to strew with owl crap. But even bringing an owl into existence, making it fly, bringing into existence the hall wherein its flight occurs: I could have done these things, too. I can do many things, albeit only in a limited space.

(*She—it is a woman—wiggles her fingers ever so slightly.*

A door opens stage left and a man enters who then walks to center stage; he has an adorable monkey face: it's Sami, back from the dead. Another door opens stage right; enter a second man, all velvet, brocade, and frogging: it's the king's son; he holds a pair of gloves filled with flowers, which he offers to Sami on bended knee.)

End quote.

— Yes, well, none of that can hold a candle to a good, licentious story. And even though yours was scarcely worthy of the name . . .

— Worthy of which name: good, or licentious?

— Either, hardly. Just the same, I was sorry to see you scuttle it. The characters were engaging, Melchior Martigon included.

— Thank you.

— If you don't mind my asking, why didn't you write it?

— I did write it, up to a point: exactly as I read it to you, that's how I wrote it.

— I mean really write it. Instead of that long-drawn-out text—with that public reading, which is so absurd, and such a bore—why didn't you simply write the book version of the story?

— Simply? Because it was, as it happens, anything but simple. Besides, the version I gave you was toned down considerably.

— Toned down? In what way?

— In many ways. And, to confine myself to technical questions, I was thinking of weaving into the plot an idea that has, for a host of reasons (all of them admittedly quite mysterious), always fascinated me, namely: someone knows the truth about another person's life, which they don't know themselves. In this case, some-one—a young woman, Miss Trellis (that's her name)—knows the truth about Aline's death. She writes to Tancred. Her letter to Tancred makes up the entirety of the book.

— Why didn't you follow through with it?

— I loathed that woman. To slog through a whole book—to spend a whole book writing in the voice of a woman I loathed as much as that? Because, make no mistake, she really was loathsome. I won't say she was planning to blackmail Tancred, exactly, though indeed she could have: he was a celebrated painter, of whom people knew nothing except that a tragedy of some sort had cast a pall over his early years. She (Miss Trellis): "A tragedy? In a pig's eye! A tawdry affair, more like (though still tragic)!" So no, she wasn't planning to blackmail him, only to drop dark hints about the potential threat: to revel, viciously and with impunity, in this implied threat—there's Miss Trellis for you!

Now, add to this the fact that the reader is not Tancred: the feelings awakened in the latter by the resurfacing of an event from his distant past, an event that had lain buried for so long, but which was no less a major turning point in his life and a profound influence on his work, though one indecipherable to everyone save Miss Trellis, who stands in possession of the facts—and to Thérèse and Melchior, of course, who have since died—these feelings the reader cannot conceive: the reader sees only the letter; Tancred's reaction on reading it can never be known.

Yet, oddly enough—it would have given Miss Trellis, at least, quite a shock (all that trouble for nothing!)—Tancred doesn't react: he's too old now, it was too long ago, the facts—the events at Thérèse's house—are nothing to him in comparison with their transfiguration in his work. The facts consisted of Aline's vision, or the absence of her vision: that she was there, still seeing the moment *before*, a moment indefinitely prolonged in the minor details of the scene; or that she hadn't been there, hadn't seen anything she wasn't strong enough to see, that she had never fallen, pulling Thérèse's dresses down with her, and that the dresses might still be visible, hanging ghostlike; or that there had been nothing and no one to see. These facts *are* his work.

Perhaps. The old lady won't say it in so many words, but she'll offer it as a hypothesis. In this version, we don't read Miss Trellis's letter directly, we get it only in the form of long excerpts quoted from memory by the old lady (she having lost the letter itself). This old lady knows nothing about Aline apart from what she's gleaned from the letter. She is Tancred's widow, speaking to an unnamed young biographer. She wonders if it's really worthwhile reopening old wounds. I, for one, think not. End quote.

— In Miss Trellis's version, or the old lady's, for that matter . . .

— But I told you, I'm never going to write this story. Beyond what I've read to you tonight, I'm never going to write any of it. I gave it up: I loathed Miss Trellis too much, as I've said, and the old lady . . . the old lady, I loved too much. I became very attached to her: her playful wisdom, her skepticism tempered with compassion. It was she, for instance, who said (in this version, she's the only speaker): "We can't rule out the possibility that Tancred, years later, and, yes, most likely in remembrance of that young woman, painted the room such as he imagined it might have looked from the transom, thereby discovering a certain treatment of space, a certain tone, which he henceforth made his own. As for the subsequent repetitions of the same space, of the motifs pertaining to this same space, could it be he was staying true to that first canvas he painted in what he would later adopt as his style? True to the painter he was becoming, rather than to the young man he had been? Simply put, could it be he was drawing inspiration from his ever more imperfect memory, from the diligent recollection of a single place?—the *place*, you understand, not the event that happened there, with which he'd already made his peace. Thérèse's house: the abstract space of his work. Such lovely light it had. Such a lovely house."

I found much to love, too, in this somewhat soft-pedaled interpretation, which had what I considered the great virtue of not saddling the subject with a pat, reductive causality (a given life leads to a given body of work) that would have been so unsatisfying to me. Where was I?

— The old lady. And that you weren't going to finish it.

— She was indeed very old, and Tancred was long dead. Assuming he'd ever lived.

— What's this? You mean to say she fabricated Tancred?

— And Aline, and Melchior, and Thérèse. And Miss Trellis. And the biographer (like me, she prefers to imagine the biographer as a woman, or perhaps a young Englishman). It was all a lie. A hackneyed device, as I'm sure I don't need to tell you, on par with "The sleeper awakes: it was all a dream," or "The author puts down his pen: it was all a book."

The fact remains, from that day forward I couldn't get her out of my mind, that old woman, that mad old woman who had fabricated it all. I no longer wanted to write any book in which she didn't appear in the final pages, pacing back and forth in her room—her little room in the nursing home—calling on an imaginary young woman to back her on some point; summoning up, with an occasional, graceful gesture of her hand, shades of the dead who had never lived; the cultivated speech, laced with archaisms, that had always been hers; her sporadic laughter—there are words and manners ingrained in one's memory which it is a form of piety to recall in laughter—the heartbreaking inflections of her voice, once magnificent, now cracked and broken with age; her solitude; her delirium.

(*He rises and begins pacing back and forth on the stage. He acts out—in a virtuoso manner, playing his part to the life—the role of the old woman. He is the old woman, the mad old woman.*)

End quote.

— Does this happen a lot?

— Oh, all the time, all the time. Except when she's asleep, and even then—I think sometimes it comes over her even in her sleep: she talks in her sleep. But there's no cause for alarm: it doesn't represent any deterioration in her condition. Besides, she gets so much pleasure from it.

— But what is she doing? What does she think she's doing? And what in God's name is she yammering on about?

— She's giving lectures of some sort, in which she'll play a whole range of different roles: a man, very often, or a younger woman. She's the audience, too. I think we can go in now. Mrs. Aubert-Maury? Guess who I've brought you! It's Tancred. It's your grandson, Tancred.

— Do come in. Close the quotation, Tancred.

— There's one objection I'm going to make . . .

— And there's one you're not going to make. I don't know why, but no one ever makes it, not ever, at least not to my face, though God knows people don't generally pull many punches where I'm concerned. Do they think it would be too mortifying for me? Maybe, but then other objections are just as mortifying, and I'm treated to plenty of those.

— What objection?

— Or rather (let's not shy away from the word) what criticism? They almost never criticize me for being stupid, at least not to my face. Yet I am stupid.

— Stupid? Possibly, I suppose. But no more so than the next guy.

— Oh, but I am, much more so than the next guy.

The next guy, you see, when he thinks, knows what he's thinking, and when he writes, writes what he knows he's thinking. He thinks, for example, that God creates the world, an infinitely good God, and this is what he writes. Or maybe he doesn't believe it (with good reason: God doesn't exist), and, in that case, considers himself under no obligation to look at the world *as if* God had created it in His infinite bounty. He sees that the term *as if* can't be applied to God and the creation of the world: a world not created by God is lacking the entire extension of God.

— Do you believe that sentence actually means something?

— He believes it, which is what counts. He believes this world is an utter shitshow. The thought saddens him, and he writes sad books. Thanks to these books, he feels a little less alone.

Or maybe he thinks this shitshow of a world can be made better. He rolls up his sleeves and spits on his hands. He doesn't let himself get distracted by the foolish consideration of what would become of him in a perfected world; he doesn't think, "Everything will be perfect for those who live in the perfected world, but what will it be like (and how unfair!) for those, including me, who had lived in the time *before* the world's perfection?" Nor does he indulge in what are essentially the preoccupations of idle aesthetes: "In this perfect world, where will heroes come from? Will there be no more heroes?," which would overwhelm him, forcing him to acknowledge that he *prefers* imperfection.

— It's true: you are stupid.

— I'm glad I was able to convince you, but you shouldn't have interrupted me when I was on a roll. If people interrupt me when I'm on a roll, I'm much too stupid to retrieve my train of thought.

— Either he thinks this, or he thinks that.

— Right: he thinks, this next guy, either this or that, or maybe even realizes both positions are tenable. So he vacillates, and then, in his intelligent way, he articulates his vacillations. He writes a treatise on doubt. Not me. No doubting for me. I don't vacillate. I don't waver. I hold all points of view simultaneously.

— Have you finished now? May I say something?

— Even though I haven't told you everything, even though I've stopped short of unveiling my stupidity to you in its full scope, its full majesty, yes, you may. End quote.

— Being stupid wouldn't be so bad if only you could tell a good yarn and find a sort of saving grace in the telling. The real problem is when the yarns aren't up to scratch. The licentious one is not up to scratch.

— I'm no longer considering writing it, as you very well know.

— But you did write it in the form you just read to us. Which was not up to scratch.

— Quite true: the old lady . . .

— It started as far back as the version with Miss

Trellis. In the so-called "Miss Trellis version," I noticed something that doesn't add up. You were thinking, you said, of incorporating into the plot . . .

— "Incorporating," I said? Are you sure? That surprises me.

— Or maybe "weaving in."

— Maybe, yes. Much more likely.

— You were thinking, you said, of weaving into the story the following idea: someone knows the truth about another person's life, which they don't know themselves.

— Yes. It's a classic trope. Furthermore, the one who knows the truth reveals it to the second person. The second, from the first, learns the truth about his or her own life, about a major event in his or her own life. A truth this second person had never known.

— Like Tancred does from Miss Trellis?

— Yes.

— But the true story behind Aline's death—we are talking about the true story behind Aline's death, aren't we?

— Yes.

— Tancred already knows it. He knows it all too well: he was there. Miss Trellis can blackmail him, she can threaten to go public (Tancred, indeed, is a public figure) with the truth no one *but* Tancred knows. And, of course, Melchior and Thérèse.

— You were right the first time: no one but Tancred. Melchior and Thérèse are dead. At least, no one but Tancred knows the version of events we know, the only version he himself is aware of, which he's kept a closely guarded secret and believes to be the true one. He's mistaken.

— It's not a secret?

— It's not a secret to at least one other person: Miss Trellis. Miss Trellis is, moreover, the only person who knows the whole truth. That is to say, she knows the truth about Tancred's life, about a major event in his life, which he doesn't.

— How does she know? For that matter, *what* does she know? You haven't said.

— I didn't have time. Did I tell you Miss Trellis was Thérèse's heir?

— No, I don't believe you did.

— In Thérèse's house, where the drama unfolded—of which, furthermore, she alone can recognize the traces scattered here and there throughout Tancred's paintings: the pleat of a curtain; the pattern of a rug; as well as, in its many iterations, the frame of the transom—in this house, she comes across a journal, or a bundle of letters (Melchior's to Thérèse, or Thérèse's to Melchior: Thérèse, when Melchior died, might have recovered the ones she'd sent him, or maybe she saved her rough drafts). There the story is spelled out in detail. Miss Trellis quotes liberally from the letters (or the journal) in her own odious letter to Tancred.

— Both Melchior and Thérèse were present at the scene, if I'm not mistaken (though Melchior arrived a bit later). They wouldn't bother telling each other a story they had both witnessed firsthand.

— They might, in the form of cruel allusions (they're cruel people): "You weren't so proud, dearest lady, on

the day . . .", "Wasn't it you yourself, good sir, who . . ."
And anyway, a journal would take care of it. As for what
Miss Trellis knows—that Aline didn't die in the wardrobe off Thérèse's bedroom, that Tancred was the victim
of a deception, that there was, in consequence, a double
deception: the first (though chronologically the second,
in which Tancred participated) was fooling the world,
beginning with the doctor, into believing that Aline had
died in bed (and yet, as it turns out, she really did die in
a bed)—all this forms the ending of the story. It's also
the ending of the book, of this particular work, which
is still in progress. You'll read it in the book.

— You haven't written it yet?

— No.

— Can you tell it to us? Please tell it to us.

— If I tell it to you now, you won't buy the book.
Buy the damn book. End quote.

— We can't be bothered with all your stories. What
interests *us* is the world: whether it's good or bad.

— You're asking me? You want me to pass judgment
on the world? Who am I to judge the world?

— You do judge it, nonetheless. What's your verdict?

— It's true, I do catch myself at it sometimes.

— And? Your verdict?

— My verdict is that, look, I want to love the world:
this wasn't a conscious decision, simply a personality
trait. You could almost call it a habit of mind. The habit

itself might be blameworthy, or at least hard to justify, but it's inalterable: when you're young . . .

— You're not young.

— But I have been, so I know what I'm talking about. When you're young, you identify with the world. Threatening as it is, you love it for being *merely* threatening, this world, your short memory of this world: tomorrow will become yesterday, and your memory less short. Or, rather, you identify the world with yourself, with your experience of the world. With the trifling evils you've suffered at its hands, enough to make you think you know something about evil. You're not starry-eyed, you give yourself credit for not being starry-eyed: you've seen the statistics. But, in spite of it all, you're still ablaze with enthusiasm. You say yes.

— "Yes"?

— Yes to the world's tragic beauty, yes to the worst of our dreams. Yes to staggering numbers, to far-off settings. They're not far-off to another person, they're the whole of his world; nor is it a dream, nor is he a number.

— And then, in the end, you change your mind: you say no.

— I say only that I can't make that call for another person. Not based on another's suffering, not by standing in another's shoes. Not from within the worst of my dreams come true for that other, because they have come true. Our nightmares are happening. We live in a world where, for other people out there, our nightmares are happening. And this, too . . .

(The plump jay that has, since the beginning of the event, been perched in stately fashion on the public reader's shoulder, now suddenly bursts out whistling "La Jeune Garde," immediately followed by "The Merry Month of May" and then a soldiers' song, unmistakably Germanic in character, which no one here among us knows. We can no longer hear ourselves think. The hall empties out. End quote.)

— Are you done? Was that the ending?

— Yes.

— So it is, in your view, of an absolutely crucial nature?

— Or, to put it more simply, it's the crux of my idea, yes.

— In that case, could we go back to a random passage . . .

— There are no random passages: all are equally essential.

— Could we go back . . .

— . . . because all form part of the same system of thought: they are the progress, albeit through many tortuous paths, of a single system of thought.

— Following your thought in its tortuous progress . . .

— Tortuous only because of the paths, is that understood?

— Understood. I was particularly struck by a passage in which you say . . .

— A passage no more or less essential than any other, correct?

— To be sure. I'm referring to the passage in which you say, on the subject of happiness . . .

— You liked that one? I'll reread it to you now!

— No, no, please don't trouble yourself.

— Oh, it's no trouble at all! It would be my pleasure. Begin quote.

(He rereads the passage, immediately followed by the ensuing "discussion," then the next discussion, and the next, until he arrives at the point where he came in: "Oh, it's no trouble at all! It would be my pleasure. Begin quote," and da capo. Fewer people notice this than might be expected, because one by one everybody present has been nodding off to sleep. At last, not wanting to disturb their slumber, the reader tiptoes off stage; when he reaches the door, he turns and looks back.)

(whispered)

— End quote.

— That's a lovely ending.

— It's not the ending. This is a work in progress. Can't you see that everything's been left up in the air? Happiness, for example: have we settled the question of happiness?

— It seems to me we have, yes: its evanescent nature, that it's under the aegis of time, that it is time.

— OK, OK, I'll give you happiness. But what about the world? The world's cruelty? How far did we get with the world's cruelty? And with the idea that, cruel as it is, some people manage to love it anyway?

(*We're in for it now.*)

— What if there were several different times? Several different orders of existence? Different orders of existence corresponding to different times?

— All coexisting? A lovable world *and* a cruel world?

— Or several.

— Several lovable and cruel?

— Yes.

— Some lovable, others cruel?

— Yes.

— But still one?

— Yes.

— But surely not lovable *insofar as* they are cruel.

— Not insofar as, no, with a few exceptions.

— *Suave mari magno* . . .

— Yes.

— And also insofar as they're made into narrative?

— Insofar as they're made into objects of narrative. Insofar as they're contained, maintained, and retained within its secular liturgy.

— And also within the aspect of its loss . . .

— Or for having been *merely* threatening . . .

(*No, it could not exactly be said they held a proper dis-cussion, though they did make a valiant effort at first. In reply to the sham objections leveled by one at some view newly advanced by the other, the latter would at once sup-ply the very response the objector himself would have given, except in those rare instances when neither the one nor the other had a ready response, instances that do not appear, or scarcely appear, in the present transcript, which records only the initial stages of the harmonious dialogue seemingly destined to continue beyond the narrow confines of this dreary hall, until such time as the death of one (the man, as it turned out) should bring it to its end. This end having arrived, the woman returned, alone, and resumed the read-ing of a text whose slant was now considerably changed.*)

— Nightmare-ridden nights, anxiety-ridden days: magnificent rough drafts, and misery was not content to stop there . . .

— We don't see the change.

— In style? That should come as no surprise to you, since the text clearly states, or at least strongly implies, that the late Albert, my husband/lover (*in order to accommodate any possible superstition on the reader's part, she will be left free to choose between the two terms: if she has a husband, she can say* my lover; *if she has a lover, she can say* my husband; *if she has both—well, does she think they're going to live forever?*), that Albert and I are one.

AUDIENCE MEMBER No. 1

May I cut in here?

THE READER
(*overwhelmed*)
Go on. At this point . . .

AUDIENCE MEMBER No. 1
I don't get it. The reader's not the author?

THE READER
The reader just told you: she and Albert are one.

AUDIENCE MEMBER No. 1
Right, but is Albert really the author?

THE READER
Ah, that I don't know. You'd have to ask the author.

AUDIENCE MEMBER No. 2
(*actually the author, who came to the reading incognito*)
Provided, that is, it's not Albert.

AUDIENCE MEMBER No. 1
Why "provided it's not Albert"?

INCOGNITO AUTHOR
Because he's dead, bozo.

(*It's true, Albert is dead. And to think they had forgotten it! Ungovernable grief and remorse assail every countenance. The author calls for a minute of silence, after which he ends the quotation.*)

— A few words, if you don't mind, about the story that was, ah . . . .

— Licentious? *The Transom*? But I told you: the ending won't be revealed tonight, or at this venue.

— I know, but by tomorrow we'll have forgotten it: we'll have forgotten how it started, we won't give a damn anymore how it ends, and we're not going to buy the book anyway.

— You're absolutely sure?

— One hundred percent.

— Well, in that case . . . It's pretty straightforward: Aline goes to Melchior Martigon's, and it's at Melchior Martigon's she dies. Not at his country house, though: in Paris, at his pied-à-terre. She dies in his bed, which is no bed of roses for Melchior. He bundles her into his car and drives to Thérèse's place, knowing Tancred won't be there yet. Together, Melchior and Thérèse carry her up to the wardrobe room. Aline sees nothing through the transom after all, not because there's nothing to see, but because she's already dead: there among Thérèse's dresses, she will never have been anything *but* dead. Happy now? End quote.

(*The reader is getting ready to leave: as he said, he has a train to catch. His gloves are still on the table.*)

— Sir! Sir! You forgot your gloves . . .

— I didn't forget them. Here, take them, I offer them to you. End the quotation, my bright beauty . . .

— I call bullshit on your story. It makes no sense!

— My story?

— *The Transom!* No sense at all!

— Oh? In what way?

— In every way. In no way. It makes no sense in any way.

— But how so? Please explain.

— You're the one who should be explaining. Explain to us a little about what you were trying to pull with this hoax, for instance.

— In the story?

— Of course, in the story.

— There are two hoaxes in the story, two deceptions: one practiced on Tancred alone, the other on the world at large.

— But the second one cancels out the first: the girl did die in bed.

— In the second one, "the girl" (she has a name: Aline) dies at a friend's house—a woman's house, moreover. It was important that, officially, she not die in Paris, at Melchior's, in Melchior's pied-à-terre: she was under twenty-one, for one thing, which made her a minor; for another, how could he ever tell Tancred what had happened, the real story of what had happened? If you were

Melchior, you'd know how Tancred would take the news
and what kind of help he'd offer you then. Fortunately
for Melchior, you aren't.

— Fair enough. But why the transom?

— Just as she couldn't very well remain at Melchior's
place in Paris once deceased, Aline couldn't just turn
up out of the blue on, say, Saturday morning, for the
sole purpose of expiring in an unexceptionable bed at
Thérèse's house: on Saturday morning, at least as far
as Tancred knew (because, in this sense, he too was
being duped by Aline) she was in Paris with her family.
There had to be some pretext for her going to Thérèse's
sooner than she'd planned (she was supposed to arrive
on Sunday), some motive inducing her to go. Making
this motive the cause of her death would kill two birds
with one stone. The pretext would be jealousy.

— She wasn't jealous, then, in actuality?

— Poised as she was to succumb—in every sense of
the word—to Melchior's potent charm, she no longer
gave a tinker's damn for Tancred.

— Another thing: wouldn't Thérèse and Tancred have
seen her face at the transom, through the glass?

— You mean, won't they find it odd—won't Tancred,
in any case, find it odd—that they hadn't seen it?
Indeed, there was no chance of them doing so, because
at no point was Aline's face ever at the transom. No, he
doesn't find it odd: the transom is high up, out of range
of the little bedside lamp; besides, it was dark inside the
wardrobe.

— The body of a person who died several hours ago

in bed wouldn't be anything like that of a person who'd just dropped dead that minute. And from falling off a stepladder.

— Aline doesn't die *from* falling off the stepladder, she ostensibly falls *as* she dies, which isn't the same thing. When Thérèse and Tancred discover her (when Tancred discovers her and Thérèse pretends to discover her), what registers with Tancred is only Aline's presence, and her death, an event that cannot be reduced to the sum of its parts. As for rigor mortis, Tancred is no Fragonard: he doesn't know the first thing about cadavers. This, however, will be one of the arguments Miss Trellis employs, years later, to convince him: "Don't you recall the position of the body? Were her arms flung wide, as if in her final moments she'd been scrabbling at the air in a vain attempt to catch herself? Were her hands clutching her failing heart? Or was she, instead, simply reclining on the floor, as shortly before she had been reclining in bed, except now with the addition of a stepladder on top of her?"

— She'd have had to be fully clothed when they found her, wouldn't she? Was she fully clothed in Melchior's bed?

— Melchior dressed her. It was the first thing he did. He had very little difficulty: her body was still pliable.

— And no problems with the autopsy? A lot of time had passed . . .

— This was a countryside very close to Paris. And Melchior drove like a speed demon, you can be dead certain.

— So to speak.

— So to speak. By the next morning, a few hours more or less wouldn't have made any difference. And there was no autopsy. It was natural causes. Aline was known to have had a weak heart.

— Was it Thérèse who heard the noise? In the wardrobe, I mean. Or at least pretended to hear it?

— Both Tancred and Thérèse heard it. There was a loud crash.

— What crashed? The stepladder? It couldn't have been Aline who knocked it over: she was dead.

— No, it was Melchior. Melchior was in the wardrobe with the dead Aline. He knocked over the stepladder. He knocked it to one side of Aline so as not to bruise the body, then quickly repositioned it on top of her.

— And what next?

— What next?

— What did Melchior do next?

— I would have liked it if he could have stayed secreted there among Thérèse's dresses, waiting for the right moment to slink away, but I needed him too soon afterward. He slunk away immediately.

— But how?

— I think I mentioned that this wardrobe had two exits: the door with the transom led to Thérèse's bedroom. Another door communicated with the servants' corridor, and was for the use of the lady's maid, enabling her to put away clothes and linens without disturbing *madame*. It was through this door Melchior made his escape. He didn't go far: he circled around to the front of the house and rang the bell.

— But Thérèse—or at least Tancred: wasn't Tancred panic-stricken by the sound of the doorbell?

— It was Melchior's trademark three short rings, which Thérèse had been expecting (this was something else they'd arranged in advance). Thérèse simply said, "Thank God! It's Melchior. Melchior will know what to do." (She understood better than anyone that he would.) You know the rest. End quote.

— And that's the end of the book? You said as much: it ends with the end of *The Transom*.

— Did I? At any rate, it is the end, yes: it has ended; it ends there.

— And you risked your reason for that?

— Risked my reason?

— Aren't you Humbert Maury?

— His name was Albert. No. I wrote this book, wrote it in this particular form, specifically in order *not* to risk my reason in the enterprise. I was relying on the frequency of the breaks: as soon as a question began to look threatening, *BANG*: end quote.

— I'd like to know . . .

— You interrupted me, madam. Can't you see I'm reading? To continue: that my reason might be dumb-founded, confounded, and *half-foundered* matters to my work, but to all of you? Well, yes, it does matter to you: you're educated people, you've learned from books that this is the price of artistic production, and the price is what interests you. What do you want? For the author to go into a trance?

(*He goes into a trance. A sorry sight.*)

To cut off his ear?

(*He cuts off his ear. Even worse.*)

Or, at the very least, to die from some spectacularly dramatic illness?

(*He dies from some spectacularly dramatic illness. It will be up to an anonymous audience member to end the quotation.*)

— Melchior Martigon isn't here, is he?
— You mean you think that scumbag is real? And not dead (if he is real)?
— To be honest, no. Besides . . .
— He is real. As you might expect, his name isn't actually Melchior Martigon. And he was here. He left a short while ago, when he realized I knew everything and was about to reveal it. You couldn't have failed to notice his exit: he made quite a racket on his way out. He knocked over several chairs.

— The tall, elderly blind man with the dog and cane?

— The very same, madam. End quote.

— If Melchior Martigon . . .

— Him again!

— If Melchior Martigon had been here . . .

— In real life, his name isn't Melchior Martigon, of course.

— The man you called by that name, at any rate. If he'd been here . . .

— He was.

— And left?

— He wasn't that stupid. Trusting to what he perceived (we know he couldn't see) of my gentlemanly demeanor, he thought he had nothing to fear. He would have done better to leave: not that I have any intention of exposing him. Though I let drop only the subtlest insinuation of menace, this half-glimpsed threat is even now taking its awful toll on his superannuated heart: I see him slumping in his seat by degrees, and his dog . . .

(*The final words of the text will be inaudible, a dog somewhere in the audience having set up a baleful howling.*)

— What about the quotation?

— Ah, yes, the quotation! You're right, it had slipped my mind.

— Then are you Tancred? You're pretending to be, anyway.

— Tancred, no: Miss Trellis.

— Miss Trellis?!

(*Now we've seen everything. End quote.*)

The very last lines do not belong to his text, which, according to several witnesses who had prior knowledge of it, continued for several pages more. These pages have not been recovered. Someone interrupted him, where you have just seen him interrupted, in such a way as to ensure that it might plausibly be said there had been a closing discussion (however brief). According to some, it was this very act, this interruption, that triggered his blind rage. I don't believe it for a moment. He was not in a blind rage. At most, the incident merely precipitated what he'd been planning to do all along. Look, it's obvious: he had planned it. The groundwork had been laid well in advance. He'd prepared the dogs. They were seen to lie perfectly still throughout the whole (not inconsiderable) duration of the reading. Young dogs, high-spirited by nature: he must have trained them to behave like that. And, in any case, it was evident he intended to do more than just read. He had something else in store, something was going to happen, there were clues within the text itself: there was the theme, among others, of public exposure (with the difference, of course, that it would not be he who would find himself most exposed). Yes, among a number of others: that the text as a whole was building up to this, I could more than amply demonstrate if you'd permit me. No? Are you sure? You don't have time? What a shame. In that case: end quote.

— You've completely lost us. Demonstrate what? To whom? And what was it that happened?
— Why, this.

(*He snaps his fingers. The three large pointers descend upon the audience. Carnage ensues. End quote.*)

— A splendid piece of writing, don't you think? So inventive . . .
— And I was so young when I wrote it!
— You didn't write it.

— What do you mean, didn't write it? Was I improvising, then? With all that variety, all those variations,
and me breezing through it like child's play?

— You didn't write it, and you didn't improvise it.
It's not yours.

— But I can recall every word, every line . . .

— You're thinking of the wrong book. End quote.

— What was in the trunk?

— You remembered the trunk!

— Yes. What was inside?

— And on top, what was on top?

— Was there something on top? Beats me. A bouquet
of lilacs?

— Something on top that wasn't visible from in the
audience?

— A label, maybe?

— It *was* a label. Bearing my name and address. The
cab driver who brought me here carried my trunk as far
as the lobby. I went off in search of someone to take it
into the hall for me: it was heavy.

(*Suddenly, the trunk appears. The reader hefts it experi-
mentally. Yes, indeed: very heavy. She goes on:*)

In the meantime, a woman entered the lobby, walked
over to the trunk, and read the label. A little while later,
this same woman passed me in the hallway and had

no doubt in her mind that it had been my name and address she had read. It's something she'll always remember: my name and address on the label; a little while later, in the hallway, her certainty—moments that will, long after I'm gone, continue to haunt her dreams.

— For crying out loud, who are you talking about?

— I was improvising. End quote.

(*The reader is a man. A dog lies at his feet.*)

— So the young man, that was you?

— I was a young man. Which one do you mean?

— The charming young man with the lady who owned dogs.

— Creatures of make-believe, madam. The dogs belonging to that woman were, as I said, large pointers. Are you blind? This dog is a mutt.

— Now that you mention it . . .

— A specially trained mutt. I myself am blind. End quote.

— You're not blind. You just read that text.

— And, more importantly, I don't have a dog. I might have been reading in Braille.

— We'd have noticed if you were reading in Braille.

Was that a metaphor?

— No.

— Then I don't understand. I didn't understand a word of that, anyway.

— You're calling me impenetrable, aren't you? I knew this was coming. I knew people wouldn't pass up yet another opportunity to throw that in my face. God knows I've tried, though. When I don't try, I'm much more impenetrable.

— You can't be *more* impenetrable.

— I can too, and I'll prove it. I've brought along a short text which, to my eye and my ear (I wrote it for myself), really says something. What it says is in fact something about me, something true about me—it is so much the truth about me that if you came here expecting to see me publicly exposed, you won't be able to say you didn't get your money's worth, in spite of mishearing me.

— We didn't understand a word of that. Are you quite finished?

— No, I'm just getting started. Everybody listening up? Begin quote:

"Oftentimes, I attempt to see Lady Albermory through Aline's eyes. Her red velvet dressing gown, her three big dogs, which Aline in fact kept for several weeks but was not to inherit; the two inches of flesh, through Aline's eyes; the bedchamber, as seen from the transom, through Aline's eyes.

"I received this letter, the one I've mentioned several times. I could not fully understand what motives might have impelled it, or what evidence might have formed the basis for its specious theory by which I was the least likely person on earth to be gulled.

"Aline died neither in Melchior's arms nor in his bed. The day of her death did not find her in his company at all: she spent the morning with me, in Paris, and it was with me she made the journey from Paris, by car, to the vicinity of the house, where I shortly thereafter saw her in through the back door after having first unlocked it for her. It was likewise at Aline's behest that I positioned the stepladder under the wardrobe transom offering a view of Lady Albermory's bedchamber.

"Lady Albermory was awaiting me outside in the lattice pavilion—it was a beautiful spring day, a beautiful May day; I went back into the house for a moment on the pretext of telephoning Aline. I still wonder what miracle—a miracle which paled to insignificance, it's true, in light of ensuing events—could have prompted me to tell Lady Albermory I had been unable to reach Aline (that she must have either already left, or inadvertently knocked her phone off the hook); perhaps I did it because, as things fell out, I had not exchanged the smallest word with her at the back door, and, being a poor liar, I invariably seek to minimize the damage. If all had gone according to plan, Lady Albermory need never have known of Aline's presence before the following morning (i.e. that she had been there prior to the following morning; that Aline had been there as early as that afternoon, as early as Saturday afternoon, is what Lady Albermory need never have known. But she did know it, as did Melchior, though they never understood, either of them, the reasons behind it, and I, of course, never enlightened them).

"Aline had a long wait, perched on her stepladder—on a stepladder, the final hours of her life. Lady Albermory was slower in making up her mind than Aline had expected, either because, though rumored to be highly susceptible to the charm of youth—and God knows I was young—she nonetheless found me singularly deficient in this quality, or because my native awkwardness was compounded by my lack of enthusiasm—in my eyes, she was a decrepit amazon, a broken-down hag, an aging Hecate amid her hounds—or because she was endowed with a greater measure of reserve than she was generally given credit for.

"It was going on six o'clock when we entered the bedroom. I had had to wheedle her out of the greenhouse, and haggle with her again—when I saw she was not going to open the shutters, closed earlier that afternoon against the already-fierce sun—in order to switch on the lamp. All things considered, I acquitted myself rather well in the business, which is as much as to say that, for love of Aline, there was truly nothing I could not do, if she asked.

"As for the letter I was to receive years later from Miss Trellis, it attested, even in the depths of its murky fabrications, to an uncanny clarity, at least to the extent that it presented Aline, in respect to a famous line from the great Corneille, as the living—or rather dying—embodiment. Where Miss Trellis confined herself to the second hemistich, however, I would have prepended the first."

Well?

— Same as usual.

— Funny, I wouldn't have said so. End quote.

— That means you really were Tancred. Or the character of Tancred, at any rate. Did you paint the paintings?

— Why, no, I certainly didn't. End quote.

— Why, yes, I certainly did. End quote.

— Did you paint them, yes or no?

— Paint them, no. The motifs I attributed to the paintings: the transom (or window), the wardrobe, the pendent dresses, the dead woman's gaze, the moment *before*: these are the motifs found in all my books—as you may have noticed, yes?

— No, we don't give a shit. We haven't read your books.

— Hey, watch your language there: you're being recorded. Everything you say will be added to the text in the appropriate place. A little respect. End quote.

(*The reader of the text is a woman, who is also its author. She is a lady of a certain age. Two large pointers lie at her feet.*)

— Here you are with your dogs. Is *The Woman with Dogs* autobiographical?

— Lady Albermory would be very old were she around today. She was already older than I am now when I had the dogs she gave me on her departure, from which these dogs are descended. She also bequeathed me her house in France. In that house, years before, a young woman had died. She had been engaged to a painter who was once quite celebrated. Nothing in this painter's body of work recalled the dead girl. End quote.

(*She is getting ready to leave the hall. There will be no discussion. The text is still on the table.*)

— Ma'am! Ma'am! You forgot the text . . .

— I didn't forget it, I'm leaving it: I offer it to you. You'll read it on four days of the year only: All Saints', Easter, Christmas, and St. John's jubilee. End the quotation, so beautifully.

—Is there anything—like, I don't know, a message?—
that you'd say was the main takeaway of your book?

— Though it's not for me to say, yes. My message is
the following: Language in general, and literature more
particularly—literature can do many things. It can take
many paths, it worms its way into all kinds of niches
where images no longer venture, and carves out niches
for itself even within images.

— Do you think you demonstrated this in your text?

— If I did demonstrate it, or was hoping to do so, it
seems to me a response would be superfluous, and yet I
am responding. But if I've failed to demonstrate it, it's
because I express myself badly and am a bad author: the
fault lies with me, not with either language or literature.

— Is there anything else you'd like to say?

— Say, no. There's something I'd like to show you.
Come closer: it's this little bird I found in the angle of
my doorway, a sparrow—a tiny baby sparrow. I fed it on
bread soaked in diluted milk, I made a nest for it inside
this box, I . . . Oh, shit, it's dead. End quote.

— What's next? What's next? (*all the children shout in
unison*).

— No. You'll hear the rest tomorrow, if you're good.
It's too late now. Time for sleep.

— Won't you sing us a song? Just one little bitty
song?

— It'll have to be a very little one. And only one.

(*She sings:*)

> Morgenrot, Morgenrot,
> Leuchtest mir zum frühen Tod?

(*She ends the quotation.*)

(*A long time has passed since the reading began, late on a Saturday evening. It is now daybreak. There will be no discussion: the reader, a very elderly gentleman, has put on his hat and is heading toward the door.*

When he reaches it, he turns to face the audience and says, raising his hat:)

— What a glorious Sunday!

End quote.

MICHAL AJVAZ, *The Golden Age.*
The Other City.

PIERRE ALBERT-BIROT, *Grabinoulor.*

YUZ ALESHKOVSKY, *Kangaroo.*

FELIPE ALFAU, *Chromos.*
Locos.

JOE AMATO, *Samuel Taylor's Last Night.*

IVAN ÂNGELO, *The Celebration.*
The Tower of Glass.

ANTÓNIO LOBO ANTUNES, *Knowledge of Hell.*
The Splendor of Portugal.

ALAIN ARIAS-MISSON, *Theatre of Incest.*

JOHN ASHBERY & JAMES SCHUYLER, *A Nest of Ninnies.*

ROBERT ASHLEY, *Perfect Lives.*

GABRIELA AVIGUR-ROTEM, *Heatwave and Crazy Birds.*

DJUNA BARNES, *Ladies Almanack.*
Ryder.

JOHN BARTH, *Letters.*
Sabbatical.

DONALD BARTHELME, *The King.*
Paradise.

SVETISLAV BASARA, *Chinese Letter.*

MIQUEL BAUÇÀ, *The Siege in the Room.*

RENÉ BELLETTO, *Dying.*

MAREK BIENCZYK, *Transparency.*

ANDREI BITOV, *Pushkin House.*

ANDREJ BLATNIK, *You Do Understand.*
Law of Desire.

LOUIS PAUL BOON, *Chapel Road.*
My Little War.
Summer in Termuren.

ROGER BOYLAN, *Killoyle.*

IGNÁCIO DE LOYOLA BRANDÃO, *Anonymous Celebrity.*
Zero.

BONNIE BREMSER, *Troia: Mexican Memoirs.*

CHRISTINE BROOKE-ROSE, *Amalgamemnon.*

BRIGID BROPHY, *In Transit.*
The Prancing Novelist.

GERALD L. BRUNS, *Modern Poetry and the Idea of Language.*

GABRIELLE BURTON, *Heartbreak Hotel.*

MICHEL BUTOR, *Degrees.*
Mobile.

G. CABRERA INFANTE, *Infante's Inferno.*
Three Trapped Tigers.

JULIETA CAMPOS, *The Fear of Losing Eurydice.*

ANNE CARSON, *Eros the Bittersweet.*

ORLY CASTEL-BLOOM, *Dolly City.*

LOUIS-FERDINAND CÉLINE, *North.*
Conversations with Professor Y.
London Bridge.

MARIE CHAIX, *The Laurels of Lake Constance.*

HUGO CHARTERIS, *The Tide Is Right.*

ERIC CHEVILLARD, *Demolishing Nisard.*
The Author and Me.

MARC CHOLODENKO, *Mordechai Schamz.*

JOSHUA COHEN, *Witz.*

EMILY HOLMES COLEMAN, *The Shutter of Snow.*

ERIC CHEVILLARD, *The Author and Me.*

ROBERT COOVER, *A Night at the Movies.*

STANLEY CRAWFORD, *Log of the S.S. The Mrs Unguentine.*
Some Instructions to My Wife.

RENÉ CREVEL, *Putting My Foot in It.*

RALPH CUSACK, *Cadenza.*

NICHOLAS DELBANCO, *Sherbrookes.*
The Count of Concord.

NIGEL DENNIS, *Cards of Identity.*

PETER DIMOCK, *A Short Rhetoric for Leaving the Family.*

ARIEL DORFMAN, *Konfidenz.*

COLEMAN DOWELL, *Island People.*
Too Much Flesh and Jabez.

ARKADII DRAGOMOSHCHENKO, *Dust.*

RIKKI DUCORNET, *Phosphor in Dreamland.*
The Complete Butcher's Tales.

FOR A FULL LIST OF PUBLICATIONS, VISIT: www.dalkeyarchive.com

RIKKI DUCORNET (cont.), *The Jade Cabinet*.
The Fountains of Neptune.

WILLIAM EASTLAKE, *The Bamboo Bed*.
Castle Keep.
Lyric of the Circle Heart.

JEAN ECHENOZ, *Chopin's Move*.

STANLEY ELKIN, *A Bad Man*.
Criers and Kibitzers, Kibitzers and Criers.
The Dick Gibson Show.
The Franchiser.
The Living End.
Mrs. Ted Bliss.

FRANÇOIS EMMANUEL, *Invitation to a Voyage*.

PAUL EMOND, *The Dance of a Sham*.

SALVADOR ESPRIU, *Ariadne in the Grotesque Labyrinth*.

LESLIE A. FIEDLER, *Love and Death in the American Novel*.

JUAN FILLOY, *Op Oloop*.

ANDY FITCH, *Pop Poetics*.

GUSTAVE FLAUBERT, *Bouvard and Pécuchet*.

KASS FLEISHER, *Talking out of School*.

JON FOSSE, *Aliss at the Fire*.
Melancholy.

FORD MADOX FORD, *The March of Literature*.

MAX FRISCH, *I'm Not Stiller*.
Man in the Holocene.

CARLOS FUENTES, *Christopher Unborn*.
Distant Relations.
Terra Nostra.
Where the Air Is Clear.

TAKEHIKO FUKUNAGA, *Flowers of Grass*.

WILLIAM GADDIS, JR., *The Recognitions*.

JANICE GALLOWAY, *Foreign Parts*.
The Trick Is to Keep Breathing.

WILLIAM H. GASS, *Life Sentences*.
The Tunnel.
The World Within the Word.
Willie Masters' Lonesome Wife.

GÉRARD GAVARRY, *Hoppla! 1 2 3*.

ETIENNE GILSON, *The Arts of the Beautiful*.
Forms and Substances in the Arts.

C. S. GISCOMBE, *Giscome Road*.
Here.

DOUGLAS GLOVER, *Bad News of the Heart*.

WITOLD GOMBROWICZ, *A Kind of Testament*.

PAULO EMÍLIO SALES GOMES, *P's Three Women*.

GEORGI GOSPODINOV, *Natural Novel*.

JUAN GOYTISOLO, *Count Julian*.
Juan the Landless.
Makbara.
Marks of Identity.

HENRY GREEN, *Blindness*.
Concluding.
Doting.
Nothing.

JACK GREEN, *Fire the Bastards!*

JIŘÍ GRUŠA, *The Questionnaire*.

MELA HARTWIG, *Am I a Redundant Human Being?*

JOHN HAWKES, *The Passion Artist*.
Whistlejacket.

ELIZABETH HEIGHWAY, ED., *Contemporary Georgian Fiction*.

AIDAN HIGGINS, *Balcony of Europe*.
Blind Man's Bluff.
Bornholm Night-Ferry.
Langrishe, Go Down.
Scenes from a Receding Past.

KEIZO HINO, *Isle of Dreams*.

KAZUSHI HOSAKA, *Plainsong*.

ALDOUS HUXLEY, *Antic Hay*.
Point Counter Point.
Those Barren Leaves.
Time Must Have a Stop.

NAOYUKI II, *The Shadow of a Blue Cat*.

DRAGO JANČAR, *The Tree with No Name*.

MIKHEIL JAVAKHISHVILI, *Kvachi*.

GERT JONKE, *The Distant Sound*.
Homage to Czerny.
The System of Vienna.

JACQUES JOUET, *Mountain R.*
Savage.
Upstaged.

MIEKO KANAI, *The Word Book.*

YORAM KANIUK, *Life on Sandpaper.*

ZURAB KARUMIDZE, *Dagny.*

JOHN KELLY, *From Out of the City.*

HUGH KENNER, *Flaubert, Joyce and Beckett: The Stoic Comedians.*
Joyce's Voices.

DANILO KIŠ, *The Attic.*
The Lute and the Scars.
Psalm 44.
A Tomb for Boris Davidovich.

ANITA KONKKA, *A Fool's Paradise.*

GEORGE KONRÁD, *The City Builder.*

TADEUSZ KONWICKI, *A Minor Apocalypse.*
The Polish Complex.

ANNA KORDZAIA-SAMADASHVILI, *Me, Margarita.*

MENIS KOUMANDAREAS, *Koula.*

ELAINE KRAF, *The Princess of 72nd Street.*

JIM KRUSOE, *Iceland.*

AYSE KULIN, *Farewell: A Mansion in Occupied Istanbul.*

EMILIO LASCANO TEGUI, *On Elegance While Sleeping.*

ERIC LAURRENT, *Do Not Touch.*

VIOLETTE LEDUC, *La Bâtarde.*

EDOUARD LEVÉ, *Autoportrait.*
Newspaper.
Suicide.
Works.

MARIO LEVI, *Istanbul Was a Fairy Tale.*

DEBORAH LEVY, *Billy and Girl.*

JOSÉ LEZAMA LIMA, *Paradiso.*

ROSA LIKSOM, *Dark Paradise.*

OSMAN LINS, *Avalovara.*
The Queen of the Prisons of Greece.

FLORIAN LIPUŠ, *The Errors of Young Tjaž.*

GORDON LISH, *Peru.*

ALF MACLOCHLAINN, *Out of Focus.*
Past Habitual.

The Corpus in the Library.

RON LOEWINSOHN, *Magnetic Field(s).*

YURI LOTMAN, *Non-Memoirs.*

D. KEITH MANO, *Take Five.*

MINA LOY, *Stories and Essays of Mina Loy.*

MICHELINE AHARONIAN MARCOM, *A Brief History of Yes.*
The Mirror in the Well.

BEN MARCUS, *The Age of Wire and String.*

WALLACE MARKFIELD, *Teitlebaum's Window.*

DAVID MARKSON, *Reader's Block.*
Wittgenstein's Mistress.

CAROLE MASO, *AVA.*

HISAKI MATSUURA, *Triangle.*

LADISLAV MATEJKA & KRYSTYNA POMORSKA, EDS., *Readings in Russian Poetics: Formalist & Structuralist Views.*

HARRY MATHEWS, *Cigarettes.*
The Conversions.
The Human Country.
The Journalist.
My Life in CIA.
Singular Pleasures.
The Sinking of the Odradek.
Stadium.
Tlooth.

HISAKI MATSUURA, *Triangle.*

DONAL MCLAUGHLIN, *beheading the virgin mary, and other stories.*

JOSEPH MCELROY, *Night Soul and Other Stories.*

ABDELWAHAB MEDDEB, *Talismano.*

GERHARD MEIER, *Isle of the Dead.*

HERMAN MELVILLE, *The Confidence-Man.*

AMANDA MICHALOPOULOU, *I'd Like.*

STEVEN MILLHAUSER, *The Barnum Museum.*
In the Penny Arcade.

RALPH J. MILLS, JR., *Essays on Poetry.*

MOMUS, *The Book of Jokes.*

CHRISTINE MONTALBETTI, *The Origin of Man.*
Western.

NICHOLAS MOSLEY, *Accident.*
Assassins.
Catastrophe Practice.
A Garden of Trees.
Hopeful Monsters.
Imago Bird.
Inventing God.
Look at the Dark.
Metamorphosis.
Natalie Natalia.
Serpent.
WARREN MOTTE, *Fables of the Novel: French Fiction since 1990.*
Fiction Now: The French Novel in the 21st Century.
Mirror Gazing.
Oulipo: A Primer of Potential Literature.
GERALD MURNANE, *Barley Patch.*
Inland.
YVES NAVARRE, *Our Share of Time.*
Sweet Tooth.
DOROTHY NELSON, *In Night's City.*
Tar and Feathers.
ESHKOL NEVO, *Homesick.*
WILFRIDO D. NOLLEDO, *But for the Lovers.*
BORIS A. NOVAK, *The Master of Insomnia.*
FLANN O'BRIEN, *At Swim-Two-Birds.*
The Best of Myles.
The Dalkey Archive.
The Hard Life.
The Poor Mouth.
The Third Policeman.
CLAUDE OLLIER, *The Mise-en-Scène.*
Wert and the Life Without End.
PATRIK OUŘEDNÍK, *Europeana.*
The Opportune Moment, 1855.
BORIS PAHOR, *Necropolis.*
FERNANDO DEL PASO, *News from the Empire.*
Palinuro of Mexico.
ROBERT PINGET, *The Inquisitory.*
Mahu or The Material.
Trio.
MANUEL PUIG, *Betrayed by Rita Hayworth.*

The Buenos Aires Affair.
Heartbreak Tango.
RAYMOND QUENEAU, *The Last Days.*
Odile.
Pierrot Mon Ami.
Saint Glinglin.
ANN QUIN, *Berg.*
Passages.
Three.
Tripticks.
ISHMAEL REED, *The Free-Lance Pallbearers.*
The Last Days of Louisiana Red.
Ishmael Reed: The Plays.
Juice!
The Terrible Threes.
The Terrible Twos.
Yellow Back Radio Broke-Down.
JASIA REICHARDT, *15 Journeys Warsaw to London.*
JOÃO UBALDO RIBEIRO, *House of the Fortunate Buddhas.*
JEAN RICARDOU, *Place Names.*
RAINER MARIA RILKE, *The Notebooks of Malte Laurids Brigge.*
JULIÁN RÍOS, *The House of Ulysses.*
Larva: A Midsummer Night's Babel.
Poundemonium.
ALAIN ROBBE-GRILLET, *Project for a Revolution in New York.*
A Sentimental Novel.
AUGUSTO ROA BASTOS, *I the Supreme.*
DANIËL ROBBERECHTS, *Arriving in Avignon.*
JEAN ROLIN, *The Explosion of the Radiator Hose.*
OLIVIER ROLIN, *Hotel Crystal.*
ALIX CLEO ROUBAUD, *Alix's Journal.*
JACQUES ROUBAUD, *The Form of a City Changes Faster, Alas, Than the Human Heart.*
The Great Fire of London.
Hortense in Exile.
Hortense Is Abducted.
Mathematics: The Plurality of Worlds of Lewis.
Some Thing Black.

RAYMOND ROUSSEL, *Impressions of Africa.*

VEDRANA RUDAN, *Night.*

PABLO M. RUIZ, *Four Cold Chapters on the Possibility of Literature.*

GERMAN SADULAEV, *The Maya Pill.*

TOMAŽ ŠALAMUN, *Soy Realidad.*

LYDIE SALVAYRE, *The Company of Ghosts.*
The Lecture.
The Power of Flies.

LUIS RAFAEL SÁNCHEZ, *Macho Camacho's Beat.*

SEVERO SARDUY, *Cobra & Maitreya.*

NATHALIE SARRAUTE, *Do You Hear Them?*
Martereau.
The Planetarium.

STIG SÆTERBAKKEN, *Siamese.*
Self-Control.
Through the Night.

ARNO SCHMIDT, *Collected Novellas.*
Collected Stories.
Nobodaddy's Children.
Two Novels.

ASAF SCHURR, *Motti.*

GAIL SCOTT, *My Paris.*

DAMION SEARLS, *What We Were Doing and Where We Were Going.*

JUNE AKERS SEESE,
Is This What Other Women Feel Too?

BERNARD SHARE, *Inish.*
Transit.

VIKTOR SHKLOVSKY, *Bowstring.*
Literature and Cinematography.
Theory of Prose.
Third Factory.
Zoo, or Letters Not about Love.

PIERRE SINIAC, *The Collaborators.*

KJERSTI A. SKOMSVOLD,
The Faster I Walk, the Smaller I Am.

JOSEF ŠKVORECKÝ, *The Engineer of Human Souls.*

GILBERT SORRENTINO, *Aberration of Starlight.*
Blue Pastoral.
Crystal Vision.

Imaginative Qualities of Actual Things.
Mulligan Stew. Red the Fiend.
Steelwork.
Under the Shadow.

MARKO SOSIČ, *Ballerina, Ballerina.*

ANDRZEJ STASIUK, *Dukla.*
Fado.

GERTRUDE STEIN, *The Making of Americans.*
A Novel of Thank You.

LARS SVENDSEN, *A Philosophy of Evil.*

PIOTR SZEWC, *Annihilation.*

GONÇALO M. TAVARES, *A Man: Klaus Klump.*
Jerusalem.
Learning to Pray in the Age of Technique.

LUCIAN DAN TEODOROVICI,
Our Circus Presents...

NIKANOR TERATOLOGEN, *Assisted Living.*

STEFAN THEMERSON, *Hobson's Island.*
The Mystery of the Sardine.
Tom Harris.

TAEKO TOMIOKA, *Building Waves.*

JOHN TOOMEY, *Sleepwalker.*

DUMITRU TSEPENEAG, *Hotel Europa.*
The Necessary Marriage.
Pigeon Post.
Vain Art of the Fugue.

ESTHER TUSQUETS, *Stranded.*

DUBRAVKA UGRESIC, *Lend Me Your Character.*
Thank You for Not Reading.

TOR ULVEN, *Replacement.*

MATI UNT, *Brecht at Night.*
Diary of a Blood Donor.
Things in the Night.

ÁLVARO URIBE & OLIVIA SEARS, EDS.,
Best of Contemporary Mexican Fiction.

ELOY URROZ, *Friction.*
The Obstacles.

LUISA VALENZUELA, *Dark Desires and the Others.*
He Who Searches.

PAUL VERHAEGHEN, *Omega Minor.*

BORIS VIAN, *Heartsnatcher.*

LLORENÇ VILLALONGA, *The Dolls'
Room*.

TOOMAS VINT, *An Unending Landscape*.

ORNELA VORPSI, *The Country Where No
One Ever Dies*.

AUSTRYN WAINHOUSE, *Hedyphagetica*.

CURTIS WHITE, *America's Magic
Mountain*.
The Idea of Home.
Memories of My Father Watching TV.
Requiem.

DIANE WILLIAMS,
Excitability: Selected Stories.
Romancer Erector.

DOUGLAS WOOLF, *Wall to Wall*.
Ya! & John-Juan.

JAY WRIGHT, *Polynomials and Pollen*.
The Presentable Art of Reading Absence.

PHILIP WYLIE, *Generation of Vipers*.

MARGUERITE YOUNG, *Angel in the
Forest*.
Miss MacIntosh, My Darling.

REYOUNG, *Unbabbling*.

VLADO ŽABOT, *The Succubus*.

ZORAN ŽIVKOVIĆ , *Hidden Camera*.

LOUIS ZUKOFSKY, *Collected Fiction*.

VITOMIL ZUPAN, *Minuet for Guitar*.

SCOTT ZWIREN, *God Head*.

AND MORE . . .